HOME FOR CHRISTMAS

CANTERWOOD CREST

SUPER SPECIAL

HOME FOR CHRISTMAS

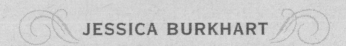 JESSICA BURKHART

ALADDIN M!X
New York London Toronto Sydney New Delhi

ALADDIN M!X

Simon & Schuster Children's Publishing Division

1230 Avenue of the Americas, New York, NY 10020

First Aladdin M!X edition November 2013

Copyright © 2013 by Jessica Burkhart

All rights reserved, including the right of reproduction

in whole or in part in any form.

ALADDIN is a trademark of Simon & Schuster, Inc., and related logo

is a registered trademark of Simon & Schuster, Inc.

ALADDIN M!X and related logo are registered trademarks

of Simon & Schuster, Inc.

For information about special discounts for bulk purchases,

please contact Simon & Schuster Special Sales

at 1-866-506-1949 or business@simonandschuster.com.

The Simon & Schuster Speakers Bureau can bring authors to your live event.

For more information or to book an event contact

the Simon & Schuster Speakers Bureau at 1-866-248-3049

or visit our website at www.simonspeakers.com.

Designed by Jessica Handelman

The text of this book was set in Venetian 301 BT.

Manufactured in the United States of America 1013 OFF

2 4 6 8 10 9 7 5 3 1

Library of Congress Control Number 2013944238

ISBN 978-1-4424-3661-9

ISBN 978-1-4424-3662-6 (eBook)

To all of those who believe in the spirit of Canterwood

ACKNOWLEDGMENTS

Seven years later and it's time to say good-bye to Canterwood Crest Academy and all of the characters who inspired me and gave me endless writing material. *runs away from computer and slinks back* This is the hardest set of acknowledgments that I've ever written.

I wish holiday cheer to each person who touched Canterwood. If I missed you in the acknowledgments, please forgive me!

Diana Peterfreund, you were the first to give me advice and tell me the NYC agent contacting me was not, in fact, a scam.

Thank you, Alyssa Eisner Henkin, for finding me and taking on my project.

Molly McGuire Woods and Rubin Pfeffer, both of you changed my life because you sought a tween horse series.

To the people on Santa's Nice List: Fiona Simpson, Alyson Heller, Bethany Buck, Mara Anastas, Lucille Rettino, Venessa Williams, Jessica Handelman, Russell Gordon, Karin Paprocki, Nicole Russo, Paul Crichton, Courtney Sanks, Valerie Shea, Craig Adams, Katherine Devendorf, Ellen Chan, Bess Braswell, Dawn Ryan,

Carolyn Swerdloff, Stephanie Voros, Deane Norton, Jim Conlin, Christina Peccorale, and Annie Berger.

Tremendous thanks to the teachers, librarians, and booksellers from Barnes & Noble to Powell's, who got Canterwood into the hands of readers.

Thanks to Cathie Morton for providing inspiration behind the racehorses-in-need story line.

To my girls, Lauren Barnholdt and Becca Leach, you've been there from book one.

Sparkles to Carrie Ryan, Aprilynne Pike, Jennifer Rummel, Melissa Walker, Marlene McPherson, Brianna Ahearn, Teri Brown, @KhloDrama, and Natalie K. Reinert.

Monica Stevenson, it's impossible for me *not* to judge my books by their covers! Thank you for shooting such striking photos again and again. Special thanks to Jill S. (aka Sasha), since you'll forever be the face of Miss Silver. Hugs to all of the Canterwood models who worked tirelessly to create gorgeous covers.

Shout-out to my Cali Barn Mafia—Joey, Lex, and Grace. Major hugs to you all!

Kate Angelella, you took over Canterwood with seamless grace. Words will never be enough (Okay, we'll go shopping!) to thank you for everything you have done for these books. They blossomed from a four-book deal

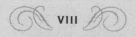

to a twenty-book series thanks to your efforts on all fronts. You've lost many things—tangible and not—while the last few books were being written and published. I hope you're able to see that not an ounce of your talent was ever diminished. I'm beyond proud to call you my best friend. LYSM. <3

Team Canterwood, I wouldn't have made it past *Take the Reins* without you. Your words of encouragement will never be forgotten. This isn't a good-bye—I hope to be writing for you for a long time! ☺

CANTERWOOD IS
COMING TO TOWN

Lauren

"OH, MON DIEU!" I SAID, LAUGHING. "WE'LL
be there in five seconds!" I glanced behind me at my
friends. Khloe Kinsella, Clare Bryant, Carina Johansson,
and Lexa Reed grinned at me from the two rows of back-
seats in the Towers's family SUV.

"There" was someplace my friends had never been.

Somewhere I was nervous to take them.

I shot a tight but excited smile to Mom, who was in
the driver's seat. I turned my gaze back to the front windshield. Mom flipped on the left blinker, and we made a
familiar turn onto my street and started cruising past
other houses in my neighborhood.

This is really happening, I thought. *There's no going back
now—you've officially brought Canterwood home for Christmas.*

My once-seedling of a dream was now reality. At first I'd thought of only inviting Carina, Canterwood's Swedish foreign exchange student, home with me to Union so she wouldn't be alone for the holiday. But my one-house-guest idea had exploded when I'd stumbled upon the *parfait* opportunity to invite all of my friends to come with me.

My BlackBerry vibrated on my lap. There was a BlackBerry message from Taylor Frost—my ex-boyfriend from home. He was a Canterwood student now too.

Taylor:

The guys & I just got 2 my house. U?

I wrote him back.

Lauren:

2 secs away from mine! ☺

A warm blush crept over my cheeks when I thought about *one* of Taylor's guests—my boyfriend, Drew Adams. He, Zack Reynolds, Garret van Camp, and Cole Harris—all from Canterwood—were en route to Taylor's house.

I was glad that Union wasn't a big town. My guy friends and Drew weren't in walking distance, but I could reach Taylor's house in five minutes via car. It felt so good to have everyone close for the holiday. All of my Canterwood friends had become more like family than I'd ever expected.

I clicked on Brielle Monaco's name. She was one of my other Canterwood friends who lived in Union.

Lauren:

U almost home?

Brielle would have ridden with us, but space was tight, so her mom had picked her up. Bri and my other bestie from Union, Ana, would be joining my friends and me for the holiday. Ana attended my old school in Union—Yates Preparatory.

Brielle:

Couple of mins away! Sooo excited!

Lauren:

Me too! :D

"Lauren?"

"Huh?" I jerked out of my thoughts when I heard Khloe's voice from the backseat.

"Is this your house?" Khloe asked.

I blinked twice and realized Mom had slowed the SUV in front of what was indeed our house. My mouth was dry—I had no idea what to say. Suddenly I was overwhelmed at having all of my friends here. I visualized having a cup of Peppermint Twist tea in front of the fireplace. Just thinking about tea calmed my nerves. I had to keep reminding myself that this Christmas wasn't about us. We had some serious work to do. My nerves evaporated. I almost wanted to jump out of the Suburban and run up to my house.

"Welcome to my home!" I said.

The girls cheered from the backseat.

2

FA, LA, LA, LA, LA!

Sasha

"THIS IS THE *BEST* COFFEE SHOP IN UNION!" I said, holding open the door for my friends.

"Thanks, Sasha," Brit Chan said. She stepped inside the Bean, and Callie Harper, Heather Fox, Eric Rodriguez, Paige Parker, and Alison Robb followed her.

My hand not holding the door was enveloped in my boyfriend's warm embrace. I glanced into Jacob Schwartz's green eyes, which set off his light-brown hair. He grinned, flashing the gorgeous smile that I loved.

"I can't believe you're here," I said. "In Union. For Christmas."

"I know," he said. "I wouldn't have missed it. I'm so happy to be here with you, Sash."

He leaned forward, pressing his soft lips on mine. I

forgot about the cold *and* the fact that I was still holding open a door. I smiled at Jacob when we pulled apart. After a breakup and makeup, Jacob and I had been back together for almost four months, and our relationship was better than ever.

"You smell like peppermint," he said.

I laughed and reached into my coat pocket, producing candy-cane-flavored lip gloss.

Jacob shook his head, grinning. "Should've known! You probably have an entire Christmas collection in your purse."

Shrugging and batting my eyes innocently, I danced away from him and through the door. "Maybe!"

We joined my friends at the counter.

"There are so many yummy holiday treats!" Alison said, tossing her wavy sandy-blond hair over her shoulder. "Any faves, Sash?"

I looked up at the Bean's holiday menu. It was written on a whiteboard in red and green marker. The counter was decorated with garland and tinsel. Christmas tunes on the local radio station played overhead. The small coffee shop in the heart of Union was within walking distance of my house. It was cold outside, but not too cold that we needed a ride from my mom or dad.

"Silver?!" Heather elbowed me. "We could try every-thing on the menu by the time you tell us what's good." Heather's ice-blue eyes bore into mine, and she stuck out a hip. She'd opened her red wool coat to reveal a cream-colored chunky-knit sweater.

"Oh my God!" I stuck out my tongue at Heather. She smiled sweetly and twisted the end of her blond ponytail. "Okay, the peppermint mocha is amaze, and the gingerbread-flavored latte and the pumpkin spice cappuccinos are so good. There isn't any holiday drink from here that I don't like, honestly."

We stepped up to the counter and a tall, gangly guy with red hair and a zillion freckles smiled at us. "What can I get you?"

"Go, Brit," Eric said.

"Okay, could I have a peppermint mocha with whipped cream, please?" Brit asked the barista. My roommate dug into her gold purse and pulled out a ten-dollar bill.

"What do you want?" Jacob asked me. "I'll order and you can go grab a table."

"Thank you," I said. "That's so sweet. I'd love a pump-kin spice latte with an extra shot of espresso, please."

"You got it," Jacob said.

I smiled my thanks and joined Brit, who had her drink.

"The tables in the back are the biggest," I said.

We walked past a few people sipping drinks and reading books or the *Union Times*. The Bean had sprayed the window bottoms to look like faux snow, and someone had painted glittery snowflakes on the glass. In the back corner, a small Christmas tree with colored lights was decorated with ornaments. Presents tagged for Union Children's Hospital were nestled under the tree.

"Here?" I asked Brit.

"Perf," she said.

We took off our coats and hung them on the back of the chairs. Brit sat across from me, and soon Callie joined us. She shrugged off her plum peacoat and smoothed her baby-pink Calvin Klein sweater. The light color made Callie's mocha-colored skin glow, and her black hair looked even darker. Paige sat next to Callie, her pale skin looking snow white compared to Callie's.

"I'm *so* going to burn my mouth, but I can't wait to taste this!" Callie said. I smelled gingerbread coming from her mug covered in snowflakes.

Brit watched Callie with her almond-shaped brown eyes and winced when Callie made a *too hot!* face.

The Bean was mostly empty, and it didn't take long

before all of my friends were seated at our table.

"This is *so* weird," I said, shaking my head. "You guys—my Canterwood friends—staying with me for Christmas. I know we'll be busy, but I can't wait to show you Briar Creek."

"It's strange for me, too," Alison said. "I've never missed a holiday at home. I consider it a Christmas miracle that my parents agreed to this!"

While everyone chatted, I lost myself in thought. All of my relationships had changed so much since my first day on campus. It hadn't been too long ago that Callie and I hadn't been speaking because she'd dated Jacob behind my back. Even though we were broken up.

Paige and I, once the tightest roomies in Winchester Hall, weren't living together anymore. I'd left to move in with Brit when Paige had sided with Callie on her dating Jacob. Paige and I were newly speaking to each other, and it was a constant struggle of mourning for the best friend that I'd once had and a girl I had to start trusting all over again.

And that was just the start.

Heather and I had hate at first sight at Canterwood. She'd been the leader of the Trio—a group consisting of Heather, Alison Robb, and now ex-Canterwood student

Julia Myer. The Trio had made my life miserable for a *long* time. Now the group had disbanded, Julia had been expelled, and Heather and *I* were close friends.

Jacob Schwartz was my first crush at Canterwood. He soon was my first BF-turned-ex. Then I dated Eric Rodriguez. We broke up and I stayed single for a while, and finally Jacob and I reunited.

Brit Chan was my roomie in Orchard Hall. She was the newest to the group. Brit and Callie had an old rivalry, because both girls excelled in dressage and each wanted to shine. Callie, never one to back down about riding, had been out for blood in the dressage arena during practices and competitions.

For a long time, it had felt like nothing would ever be the same at school. Then my riding instructor, Mr. Conner, had been in a serious accident when he had been teaching my class.

That terrifying event—a horse flipping onto its back and crushing Mr. Conner's leg in front of Callie, Heather, Brit, and me—had forced us to look at what was really important. Our stupid vendettas against each other had to stop. We weren't all besties, but we were *trying*. For us that was progress.

"How could they say no?" Eric asked. He ran a hand

through his short, spiked black hair. "Sasha, you found the perfect way for us to spend Christmas. Something that embraces the holiday spirit."

Turning in my seat, I reached into my purse, dug through a handful of lip glosses, and found the flyer and e-mail I wanted. I laid them flat on the table.

Everyone peered at the flyer, even though we'd been planning this since Thanksgiving.

Be an elf this Christmas!
Safe Haven for Thoroughbreds needs your help!
If you have time, fund-raising resources, or
experience with horses, please call or e-mail us.
We're seeking volunteers for the upcoming
Holiday Adopt-a-Thon!
Call 519-555-0100

Beside the flyer was a copy of the confirmation I'd received from Lyssa, a volunteer for Safe Haven.

11/23 9:04 a.m.
To: Sasha Silver
From: Lyssa Grey
Subject: Re: Holiday volunteers

Hi, Sasha,

Wow! Thank you so much for your e-mail! My name is Lyssa, and I'm the volunteer director for Safe Haven for Thoroughbreds (SHT). It's incredibly generous of you and your friends to offer your time to help us prepare the horses for the Holiday Adopt-a-Thon.

Attached please find parental permission slips that you'll each need to bring signed. Also, there is an info sheet with the date, time, and location of our first meeting. Please wear riding boots and bring a helmet. You'll find a FAQ on our website, or contact me with any questions.

All best,

Lyssa Grey

"I think my mom was a little, like, oh my God, you won't be home to help with your siblings over break," Callie said, giggling. "Working with ex-racehorses is going to be a breeze compared to that!"

"We start on Monday. I can't wait!" Brit said. The soft lights of the Bean shone down on Brit, making her silky black hair look extra shiny.

"It'll be fun to be around horses," Paige said. "I'm glad the organization let me participate even though I'm not a rider."

"Maybe they'll get you to whip up a fab menu for the adopt-a-thon," I said. Paige was an insanely talented cook.

Paige shot me a smile. "Don't even let me start dreaming about that!"

"I feel lucky that your parents were cool with Eric and me staying at your house," Jacob said. "Not many parents would be okay with us staying with all of you girls."

I took a sip of my latte and grinned. "Oh, they were *so* not okay with it at first! My dad said, 'Absolutely not, young lady!' and I reminded him that we had extra rooms and you and Eric were totes fine with sharing one. He and my mom talked about it forever, and when they finally said yes, I thought they were going to make me sign a contract or something!"

Everyone laughed.

"Like, no kissing your boyfriend in the house," Brit said.

"Or no guys putting one toe in your room," Alison added.

"And you must remain five feet apart at all times," Callie said, giggling.

"Pretty much!" I said. "My dad kept me on the phone so long with a list of 'There will be no . . .' that my BlackBerry battery died!"

A hand slipped into mine, and I smiled at Jacob sitting

next to me. "Well, that just means I'm going to be holding your hand a lot more when we're out," he said.

"Hmmm." I tapped my cheek, pretending to consider it. "Okay!"

We finished our drinks, and my muscles relaxed from the car ride. Or maybe the stress I'd been carrying around about all of us being together. Mom and Dad had picked us all up this morning at Canterwood, and we had dropped our stuff in the living room before needing a caffeine fix. I doubted I'd need any caff, though, when we started at Safe Haven on Monday. I had already spent hours on my iPad, scrolling through the list of adoptable horses and wishing I could adopt one.

"Ready to go back to my house for a tour?" I asked. A surge of happiness went through me—there hadn't been an ounce of weirdness so far between any of us.

"Let's see your place," Heather said. She tossed me a quick smile, and it said what she didn't have to—she was glad to be here. I'd learned just how little Mr. and Mrs. Fox paid attention to their daughter when I'd visited Heather once. I wanted to make this Christmas special for her, too. There was no better place to have a magical Christmas than Union, Connecticut.

3

BIENVENUE
À LA MAISON

Lauren

"YAY!" LEXA CHEERED. "WE'RE HERE!" THE
other girls added whooping noises.

Mom parked the SUV in front of the three-car garage,
and everyone hopped out onto the driveway.

"This," I said, sweeping an arm in the direction of the
house, "is my home."

The front of our five-bedroom house was a light gray,
with dark-gray stones from the bottom to the peak. The
attic window was stained glass and one of my favorite parts
of the house. The rest of the sides had eggshell-colored sid-
ing. The lawn was browned from the cold, but the shrubs
along the sidewalk that wound up to the doorway were still
green. There were two black lampposts, one on each side of
the sidewalk just in front of the two brick stairs up to the

front door. The glass door was etched in gold, and light from inside the house spilled onto the porch.

"It's so pretty, Lauren and Mrs. Towers," Carina said. "I love it!"

"Thanks!" I said.

"It will be even better when Lauren's dad and I get out the Christmas decorations," Mom said. She made an apologetic face at me. "I'm sorry, sweetie. We didn't have time to decorate just yet this year."

Disappointment swept through me. I'd envisioned my friends walking into a Christmas wonderland.

"It's okay, Mom," I said. "I know Dad's been on a book deadline and you're busy at work."

The front door opened and my dad, Gregg, stepped outside. He was actually my stepdad, since my biological father had died just after I'd been born. But Gregg was the only dad I'd ever known, and we were *très* close. The weirdest thing? Even though Dad and I weren't blood related, we both had the exact same color eyes—pale blue. It was one of those cool things that I was glad we shared.

"Bell!" Dad called, hurrying down the steps and sidewalk. Dad had called me "Bell" or "LaurBell" ever since I could remember. He was in his usual writer clothes— jeans and a sweater, and he'd thrown on a black coat.

"Dad, hi!" I grabbed him in a huge hug, and he spun me around.

"Hi, girls," Dad said, putting me down and smiling at my friends.

"Hi, Mr. Towers," everyone said politely.

"Please, call me Gregg," Dad said. "That 'Mr. Towers' stuff makes me feel old."

My friends grinned.

"Let's get you girls inside," Mom said after she kissed Dad's cheek.

We grabbed as much luggage as we could carry, and I was the first one to the door.

"Here it is," I said. I turned the gold knob, pushed open the door, and gasped.

My friends momentarily forgotten, I stepped through the doorway. Seasonal smells of pine, cinnamon, clove, and peppermint hit my nose. The living room was covered in Christmas decorations, and in the back of the room near the sliding glass door, a giant tree twinkled with colored lights.

"*Oh, mon Dieu!*" I said, turning around. "Mom! Dad! You said you didn't decorate!"

Lexa, Clare, Khloe, and Carina peered around me, trying to see inside. Mom and Dad grinned at me over their heads.

"We didn't have time to decorate the *outside* yet," Mom

said. "Of course Dad and I wanted you and your guests to come home to a houseful of Christmas cheer."

"Ahhh! C'mon in, guys!"

We all scurried through the doorway, and I motioned for everyone to put down their bags.

"Wow, it smells *insane* in here!" Khloe said.

Mom tilted her head. "Is that good or bad?"

Khloe laughed. "It's *very* good!"

We all laughed as we took off our shoes and put them in the closet. Dad took each of our coats and hung them in the same closet.

"Your dad and I have some work to do," Mom said. "Please make yourselves at home. The kitchen is full of snacks and drinks, and Lauren will show you around. We're so happy to have you all!"

"Thank you so much!" Clare said, her long red waves bouncing around her shoulders. The rest of the girls added their thanks, and my parents disappeared. I knew from an earlier BBM that Becca, my older sister, wasn't going to be home for a few more hours.

"Grab your bags and I'll show you the guest room," I said. "You can decide where you want to stay."

Khloe gave Clare a pretend evil eye. "I refuse to room with Bryant. She snores."

Clare punched her best friend on the arm. "Please. You recite lines in your sleep from whatever script you're studying."

Khloe smiled. "I'm a true, dedicated actress, obviously."

"Let's take this discussion this way," I said, sticking out my tongue at them.

We climbed the stairs to the second floor. Garland wrapped around the banister, and white lights were nestled in the greenery. I led my friends to the guest room. Ellen, our part-time maid, must have just cleaned, because the room smelled lemon fresh. The white bedside table had a bowl of pinecones covered in red and green glitter. A painting of the New York City skyline hung above the bed on the off-white wall. The bed was made up with a red down-filled comforter and dark-brown sheets. The open blinds let the bleak December sun cast a little light in the room.

"I was thinking that Khloe and Clare could take the bed in here, since it's a king," I said. "Is that okay?"

Khloe and Clare nodded.

"Absolutely," Khloe said.

"Under the window, that's a daybed that my parents got just for you guys." I nodded to the white-wire bed frame with a mattress covered with a seasonal white comforter with light-blue snowflakes. "Lex, I was thinking that bed could be yours."

"It's so cute!" Lexa exclaimed. She hurried over to the bed and put her luggage beside it. "Taken!"

I looked at Carina. "My mom said there's another one of those set up in my room, if you're okay bunking with me."

Carina smiled. "That sounds great, Lauren."

I wanted Carina to share my room because I was closer to her than she was with the other girls. Plus, it had been my original intention to only invite her.

"You guys unpack—feel free to put your stuff in the dressers and closet—and I'm going to take Carina to my room. It's at the end of the hallway to the right. So come find us when you're done."

"Thanks so much, LT," Khloe said. "This is a great room."

"Agreed," Clare said.

"I think Lexa would say the same," I said, laughing. Lexa had plopped on top of the daybed and was stretched out, her face buried in the pillow. She mumbled something unintelligible.

Smiling, I left my friends, and Carina followed me to my room.

"That's my sister Becca's room," I said, pointing. "And

this one is Charlotte's—my oldest sister. My parents' room is on the first floor."

"Are your sisters going to be here?" Carina asked.

"Yes. Becca's only two years older than me, so she lives here. She'll be home later today. Charlotte is at college, but she's coming home for break. She's flying home on Tuesday."

We reached my room, and I pushed open the half-closed door.

"Lauren!" Carina said. "Oh, *wow!*"

I couldn't stop the feeling of pride that built in my chest. Only Ana and Brielle had been in my room before. It was a huge relief that at least one of my Canterwood friends liked it.

We put down our bags and Carina wandered around, looking. "Did you decorate this yourself?" Carina asked.

"Yep," I said. "I like soft colors and clean lines. Kind of classic American in my favorite color—pale blue."

A floor-length mirror was framed in twisted metal painted ivory. Icy-blue velvet curtains were drawn back from my windows. My bed had one of my favorite comforters—a soft white with flower outlines stitched in blue. A white ladder bookcase rested along one wall next to my desk.

Along the wall near the bathroom door was the second daybed—this one had the same white metal frame and a micro-fleece lavender comforter and a stack of pillows.

"This is the closet," I said, tapping on the door. "Please use it so you're not living out of a suitcase." I flipped on a light. "And this is our bathroom."

Carina poked her head inside. "It's *so* chic! This is totally you, Lauren."

"Thanks!"

The bathroom had alternating white and blue towels hanging off a rack. A plush suede chair was tucked under a low part of the counter, where I usually did my hair and makeup. The shower curtains, ones I'd been thrilled to find, were blue-and-white pinstriped.

"It'll be so fun with you in here," I said. "But if you don't want to be in this room or if you want to bond with the girls by staying in the guest room, it won't hurt my feelings."

Carina gave me a tiny smile. "Honestly? I was a little intimidated with the idea of staying with the others, since I *do* know you better. I adore your room and am so happy in here!"

"Yay!" I said. "Want to unpack so that's over?"

Carina nodded and with that, we unzipped our

suitcases and clothes started flying into the closet. We had just finished when Khloe, Lexa, and Clare walked into my room.

They added how much they liked my style, and before my ego exploded, I suggested we go downstairs for snacks and a tour of the rest of the house. I could barely contain my excitement—this was going *way* better than I'd hoped! And Ana and Brielle weren't even here yet.

4

CANTERWOOD, MEET BRIAR CREEK

Sasha

I WOKE UP *WAAAY* TOO EARLY THE NEXT morning, but I was too excited to sleep! It felt a little strange to wake up at home instead of in the dorm room that I shared with Brit at Canterwood.

I was taking my friends to Briar Creek this morning. Everyone would get to meet Kim and see my old stable. Nerves stabbed my stomach. All of my friends knew that I'd started at a tiny stable, but they hadn't *seen* it. Would they think less of me after we went to BC?

No, I told myself, rolling over on my side. Callie was sound asleep on an air mattress, the blankets kicked off, revealing candy-cane-covered pj's. I loved having my friends here. Although it had been a little, okay, a *lot* scary showing Jacob my room yesterday. But he seemed to like my shelf of Breyer model horses, bookcase stuffed with horse books, and the bulletin board that was filled with photos of my friends and Charm.

I slipped out of bed and threw a bubble-gum-pink robe over my purple plaid pajamas. I eased open my door and peered down the hallway. The door to the boys' room was still shut, and the den where Brit, Alison, Paige, and Heather were sleeping was dark. I tiptoed down the hall and to the bathroom to wash my face and start to get ready for Briar Creek.

I rubbed my eyes, turned the corner, and—"Ahhh!" I shrieked.

Jacob's green eyes stared into mine. He steadied me with his hands on my elbows.

"Sorry!" I said, giggling. "Are you okay?"

His hair was sticking up and his eyes were sleepy. "You *did* bodycheck me at eight in the morning." He grinned. "But I think I'll survive."

The second Jacob said "morning" I realized that *I* was in pajamas. And so was Jacob! I couldn't stop myself from checking out his flannel blue-and-gray-striped pants and long-sleeve shirt. I pulled my eyes to his face, simultaneously yanking my robe tighter across my body.

"Um, well, I—I've got to get ready!" I said, hurrying

around him. I couldn't even think about what a morning mess I had to look like.

"Cute pj's, Sash!" Jacob called playfully.

With a squeak, I darted into the bathroom. *Okay,* I told myself. *No more leaving the bedroom in the morning unless I'm fully dressed and at least semi-presentable.*

I flipped on the light and squeezed my eyes shut when I got in front of the mirror. Slowly, I opened one eye and then the other.

"Omigod! Are you kidding me?! Omigod!" I grasped the counter and stared at my reflection.

Last night Callie and I had done Bioré blackhead strips on our noses. Apparently, *I* had fallen asleep with mine on! The stiff white strip made me look like I was recovering from a nose job.

"Ugggh!" I groaned, ripping off the strip and leaving a Rudolph red nose behind. Of course I'd run into my boyfriend with *that* stuck to my face. Obvi, I had a lot to learn about having temporary guy roomies.

A couple of hours later, everyone had dressed and eaten eggs and pancakes that Mom had made, and Dad was at the wheel of the SUV, slowing as we pulled into Briar Creek's driveway.

Heather had claimed shotgun, and she leaned forward, peering through the windshield. It was a gray December day, but there wasn't a threat of snow. I took a Lip Smackers from my coat pocket and smoothed on the holiday pomegranate-flavored gloss.

"This is it," I said, my voice small.

Kim had done a lot of renovation since I'd left. The stable had attracted more students after I, and then Lauren Towers, had trained here and been accepted to Canterwood. The pastures on either side of the driveway had freshly painted fences. The old orange round pens that had rusted at the hinges were gone. In their place—a new arena. The stable, once sporting chipped paint, was now a glossy gray.

Dad eased the Ford to a stop at the stable entrance. "Call me when you're ready to come home," he said to me.

"Okay, thanks, Dad," I said.

Heather got out, and I hopped to the ground, followed by Brit, Paige, Callie, Jacob, Alison, and Eric.

I shoved my hands in my pockets, almost unable to breathe as I waited for the verdict from my friends.

"Briar Creek is so great," Alison said, her eyes roaming over the grounds. "It feels so intimate. I love that."

I grinned. "Thanks, Alison."

"It really looks like a good place to train," Heather said. She held up her hands in a *what gives?* gesture to me. "You made it sound like we were coming to a place with rusty barbed-wire fences and overflowing muck piles. What's that about?"

Everyone looked at me. "I don't know," I said, shrugging. "I guess I didn't want you guys to expect something like Canterwood and be disappointed. This place is really important to me, and I wanted my friends to like it as much as I do."

"Well, *I* think it's fab," Brit said, looping her arm through mine. "I want to meet the horses!"

"Yeah, I want to see the stable!" Callie said. "Come on, Tour Guide."

Laughing, I led them inside. The stable was empty, as it usually was during Christmas break. I was glad to have the place to myself to give my friends a private tour. I'd texted Kim to tell her we were coming, and I couldn't wait to introduce her to everyone.

"Ooh, a Morgan just like Black Jack!" Callie said. She broke free of our cluster and headed for a stall up ahead. The black horse had his head over the stall door, his muzzle stretching toward Callie. "Aww! He's so sweet! You'd like my horse, Jack," Callie told the Morgan.

Kim had added on stalls and more space at the back of the stable. I'd seen photos that she'd sent me when the construction was finished. Now there were about thirty stalls.

I gave everyone a tour, showing them the tack room, Kim's office—empty but with the desk light on—and the feed room, and we leisurely started down the main aisle to look at the horses.

"I *did* ask Kim if we could borrow stable horses to trail ride whenever we have free time," I said. "She said yes and sent me a list of the horses that were going to be available to us."

"Awesome," Eric said. "I'll miss Luna, but I'm glad I get to ride."

Luna was the sweet gray Canterwood mare that Eric rode. When Eric and I had dated, Luna had acted as if she had a crush on Charm. The two horses were still good friends. Just like Eric and me.

I turned to Jacob. "Kim's got a very quiet, easygoing horse picked out for you," I said. I nodded at Paige. "Same for you. You guys don't *have* to ride, though. If you don't want to, I'll stay back with you and we can hang out."

Jacob smiled and threaded his fingers through mine. He wasn't an equestrian, but he had basic knowledge of riding. His teacher had been none other than Eric, my ex-boyfriend, who had so generously taught Jacob in secret so he and I could ride together.

Paige's experience around horses was limited too, and she'd never had lessons.

"I trust that you chose the right horse for me," Jacob said. "You know what I can handle. Plus, I want to spend time with you, and this entire break is *about* horses. I want to ride."

I squeezed his hand. "You're the best!" I gave him a quick kiss and bounced on my toes.

Jacob wrinkled his nose. "I have to say, I'm pretty good at guessing most of your lip-glossy things—flavors. But what *is* that?"

Laughing, I told him.

"Let me try it again," he said.

I kissed him, and we smiled at each other.

"I'll remember that one now," Jacob said.

"Okay!" I said, suddenly aware that everyone was watching us with grins on their faces. "Paige, what would you like to do?"

"Ride, obvi!" Paige said. "I want to. You gave me a riding lesson once, and I think I've done enough of the basic stuff with you to ride."

"Let me take you to the horses that we'll be riding. They're at the end of the stable." I worked hard to keep my steps even and not turn around and spill secret news I'd been holding inside for weeks.

5

JUST CALL ME SANTA

Sasha

MY FRIENDS FOLLOWED ME, AND I WALKED up to a stall and clicked my tongue against the roof of my mouth to get the horse's attention. The palomino gelding started toward me and put his beautiful Arabian head over the door.

I turned to the group, and Alison gasped. Her eyes were as round as peppermint candies.

"Alison," I said. "You'll be riding this strange horse named . . . Sunstruck. I think that's his name. Is that okay?"

"Omigod! Baby!" Alison ran forward toward her horse and peppered his muzzle and cheeks with kisses.

"How did you—? When did—?" Alison sputtered at me.

Eric, Callie, Brit, and Heather all shared the same look: hope. Hope that their horses were here and not at Canterwood.

"They're all here!" I said. "I coordinated the travel with Mr. Conner, and he worked with your parents and Kim. They'll be staying at Briar Creek until we go back to school."

Eric looked at his boots for a split second. "Luna's here too," I assured him. "Mr. Conner knows you love her like she's yours."

That made him grin.

"Go find your horses," I said. "They're all in the last few stalls."

Callie, Eric, Brit, Heather, and Alison hurried down the aisle, not even glancing at the Briar Creek horses.

"If it's okay, I'd like to say hi to Charm and then introduce you to your horses," I said to Jacob and Paige.

They nodded.

"That was an amazing surprise, Sash," Paige said.

"I wanted the horses to be home for Christmas too," I said. "Home for them is wherever we are."

Jacob, Paige, and I walked past Heather, who had her arms around Aristocrat's neck. The liver chestnut leaned into her. Brit had found Apollo—her gray gelding—and was whispering in his ear. Callie and Black Jack were reunited in the stall next to Apollo. Eric dug into his pocket, produced a peppermint stick, and held it flat on his palm for Luna.

It made me teary to see all of my friends with their horses—the horses they thought they'd be without over break. It hadn't been easy getting them here. The Foxes had put up a fight about having Heather's expensive horse staying "at some stable in *Union*," but Mr. Conner and I had managed to convince them.

"Charm?" I called. A low nicker came from the right side of the aisle. "Chaaarm! I hear you!" Another nicker, louder and longer this time. I broke into a jog, not waiting for Paige and Jacob to catch up.

As I reached the stall, a chestnut head popped over. Wide brown eyes found me, and I grinned. "Charm!" I wrapped my arms around his neck, burying my face in his mane. He smelled like clean hay and sweet grain. I stepped back and held his face in my hands. Charm wore his dark-brown leather halter, with his name inscribed on a gold name plate attached to the halter.

"Look at my other boyfriend," I said as Jacob reached my side.

"Hey, Charm," Jacob said. He put out a tentative hand

for Charm to sniff. Charm bumped Jacob's hand with his muzzle, and Jacob patted his neck. I couldn't believe Jacob was the guy who, when we had first met, was so scared of horses he wouldn't even touch Charm.

Paige caught up and petted Charm's cheek.

Charm's coat gleamed from daily brushings. Every hair on his white blaze sparkled like fresh snow. His socks were just as clean. Charm's breeding—a mix of Thoroughbred and Belgian—made him tall and strong.

"Anyone interested in a ride?" I called.

"Yes!" everyone chorused back.

With a final pat, I left Charm, and my friends and I met in the center of the aisle.

"Sasha, wow," Callie said. Her brown eyes danced. "This was the biggest surprise!"

Heather nodded. "Really. I was down about spending Christmas away from Aristocrat. Thank you so much!"

I waved my hand. "I wanted to do it. Mr. Conner did most of the work, really. It's a small thanks to you all for helping me with the charity project."

I explained that everyone would find their tack and grooming supplies in a closet at the back of the stable. I hadn't wanted to blow the surprise when I'd shown them the real tack room.

"So, you guys tack up. I'm going to introduce Jacob and Paige to their horses and help them get ready. Want to meet out in front of the stable in half an hour?" I asked.

"Deal!" Brit said.

6

SHADY LAUREN

Lauren

"YOU," KHLOE SAID, POINTING A RED FINGER-
nail at me, "are being shady."

We had just finished breakfast and were getting ready
to go to Briar Creek. I wanted to show my friends the
stable and go trail riding. Taylor, the rest of the guys, Ana,
and Brielle were meeting us there.

"Me?" I asked. My voice was octaves higher than nor-
mal. "Nope, no shadiness here."

Clare, in black breeches and a down vest, studied me.
"Khloe's right. Something's up."

Channel Khloe, I told myself. *Be an actress!*

"I—I was just thinking about Charlotte coming home
tomorrow," I said. "It's going to be a little weird."

Clare, Khloe, Lexa, Carina, and Becca all exchanged looks. We were seated at the breakfast nook table. The girls had met Becca yesterday, and I couldn't have asked for a better introduction. Just like I knew she would be, Becca was open and friendly with everyone, and it didn't take long before she felt like one of our group. Everyone had whispered to me the second Becca had stepped out of the room last night how much they liked her.

"Don't worry too much, Laur," Becca said. "I'm sure things with Char will be fine. You guys have really come a long way."

I thanked my sister with my eyes. Becca knew why I was distracted—and it wasn't about Charlotte. Right *now*, anyway. Late last night, I'd woken up to my phone blinking on my nightstand. In my in-box was an e-mail from Char.

12/17 1:32 a.m.
To: Lauren Towers
From: Charlotte Towers
Subject: Coming home
Hi, Laur,
*I'm taking a break from last-minute packing
and wanted to e-mail you. Texting would have*

taken forever! I guess I just wanted to say that I hope you're looking forward to Xmas as much as I am. It's going to be a little different with your friends there, but I'm glad you have people over—the charity work is especially cool. I should have told you that sooner. I'm really proud of what you're doing. I miss you (and the rest of the fam) and think this will be the first Christmas in a while that everyone— you and I, especially—are going to have fun being around each other. I want this to be a great holiday! ☺

See you very soon!

Xoxo,

Char

I'd read the e-mail three times. Charlotte was really trying. She wanted to put our rocky past behind us, at least for the holidays, and have a good time. As sisters, Char and I rarely got into screaming fights—most of our issues came from the competitive gene that we both shared. When I came home with an A– on a history quiz, Charlotte brought home an A on a math test. I excelled in riding, and Charlotte made sure she was captain of the cheer squad. Mom always said that it was because Char and I were so alike that we didn't get along. Maybe, just maybe, Charlotte and I would be a little less Grinch-y toward each other this Christmas.

"Girls? Ready to go?" Dad asked, popping his head into the room. I blinked away my thoughts of Charlotte.

"Yes!" I said. I jumped up so fast that I bumped the table and almost knocked over my half-full glass of Tropicana OJ.

Before the girls could say anything, I darted toward the foyer and the coat closet.

Dad had already warmed up the SUV and had 101.7 playing holiday tunes when we got inside.

I didn't know how I was going to make it through this ride! I pulled out my phone and texted Taylor.

Lauren:

W r on r way 2 BC. U?

Taylor:

Dad bailed at the last min from driving us so we've got our driver. Just picked up A & B.

Lauren:

☹ Sorry, T. Glad u have A & B—they'll tell u how 2 get to BC.

Taylor:

A, yes. B . . . ? Not so sure abt her sense of direction. :p

Lauren:

LOL. True. Let me know if u need help.

I locked my phone and shoved it into my stable coat pocket. I looked up and Lexa, sitting next to me, was staring.

"What?" I asked.

"Spill it," Lexa said.

"There's nothing to spill!" I said.

"Lauren Towers!" Khloe called from the backseat, leaning forward. "I'm going to . . . ask your dad to turn this car around if you don't talk!"

Everyone giggled and Dad laughed.

I couldn't take it a second longer.

"*Oh, mon Dieu!* You guys are so bad! Fine!" I shifted in my seat so I could see everyone. They all looked expectantly at me. "Becca's the only one who knows about this," I continued. "Cole, Ana, Garret, Zack, Drew, and Brielle don't. And neither does Tay—not that it impacts him really."

"Lauren!" Clare said.

"Okay, okay! I wanted to wait until we got to Briar Creek, but it really was killing me to wait. I have a little Christmas surprise for you all. Mr. Conner helped me. . . ." I paused for dramatics. Then I saw the look on Khloe's face. She was about to jump over the seat and strangle it out of me. "All of our horses are at Briar Creek!"

All the girls started talking at once.

"What?" Carina said. Her platinum hair fell over her shoulder. "Rocco is there?"

I smiled. "He is! I know your horse from home isn't here, Carina, so Mr. Conner wanted you to have Rocco, since he's the only Canterwood horse you ride."

"Omigod! Omigod!" Khloe squealed. "I won't have to wait until next year to see Ever!"

"When did the horses get here?" Clare asked. Her fair cheeks were pink.

"Last night," I said. "Kim texted me when they were unloaded and checked to make sure everyone had traveled safe. They're all waiting for us at Briar Creek."

"I knew you were up to something!" Khloe said, shaking her head at me with a smile. "I'm glad it was something like this. You know how much we wanted to see our horses during break, but we didn't need a thank-you for volunteering."

The other girls nodded.

"I would have missed Fuego like crazy," Clare said. "But I hope you didn't feel you had to do something for us or get us something for helping out."

I shook my head. "I didn't. I knew how I felt—I didn't want to spend Christmas away from Whisper, especially our first Christmas. I knew you all probably felt the same. I wanted to do this. I'm excited it worked out."

"Did Zane come too?" Carina asked. I pictured Brielle's albino gelding, who she'd bought from Kim before coming to Canterwood.

"He did," I said. "Brielle doesn't even know. Plus, Polo's here for Drew, Nero for Zack, Scout for Garret, and Valentino for Cole."

"What's Taylor going to do?" Lexa asked. "He doesn't ride."

"He knows how," I said. "I taught him enough to trail ride with us when he spent time with me at Briar Creek. Kim will pick out a *très* quiet stable horse for him."

"Riding at a new place is going to be so much fun . . . ," Carina said.

I stopped listening and took out my phone again. It was only fair to tell Cole, Garret, Drew, Zack, and Brielle, since everyone else knew.

"I'm just going to tell the others, since you guys pried it out of me," I said.

They laughed and went right back to talking about riding at Briar Creek.

I opened up BlackBerry Messenger and typed a message to Zack, Garret, Drew, Cole, and Brielle.

Lauren:

This was supposed 2 be a SURPRISE, but the girls got it out of me. ☺ I wanted all of us 2 spend Xmas 2gether. By all, I mean r horses 2. Sooo . . . B, C, G, Z, & D, you have guests waiting @ BC. Zane, Valentino, Scout, Nero, & Polo r there! Now we can ride r horses when we r not volunteering & spend Xmas w them. ☺

I sent the message, watched as it got read, and messages came back almost simultaneously.

Drew:

R u srs?!

Cole:

OMG, LT! U r my Xmas angel!

Garret:

You sneak! ☺

Zack:

Good 1, LT!

Brielle:

NO WAY!!! ☺ ☺ ☺

I typed another message to them.

Lauren:

See u v soon! ☺

I looked up from my phone, and Dad was pulling

in front of the stable. The girls chattered about the grounds and I listened, not saying a word. Having my Canterwood friends here felt surreal. Briar Creek had been the place where I had made the decision to ride again after my accident. It had been the stable where I had gone through a rehab of sorts—helping me with my fears of jumping and slowing the flood of memories from my fall at Red Oak.

Briar Creek was the place where I had met Kim. She had been encouraging, tough, kind—everything I'd needed to get to a place to apply to Canterwood.

More important than anything, Briar Creek was where I'd brought Whisper after I'd found her. This stable was the first place we had really bonded, and I'd never forget it. Nor would I forget that it had been Kim and her contacts who had led me to Whisper. I couldn't imagine my life without my sweet gray mare. If I never got another Christmas present again, I could honestly say I would be happy. Even though I was excited to start volunteering tomorrow, I was glad to have a Sunday afternoon with Whisper.

Dad was speaking, but it sounded garbled. The SUV doors opened, cold air flooding inside, and I sat frozen in my seat. The girls piled onto the driveway and gravel crunched as Taylor's driver pulled an Escalade up next to us.

I flicked my eyes to the rearview mirror and caught Dad staring back at me. His look reassured me that I'd made the right choice in bringing everyone here.

"You've got this, LaurBell," Dad said. "Go show everyone who and what made you the girl you are."

"Thank you, Dad." I unbuckled my seat belt and leaned over the driver's seat to hug him. "I love you and I'll call you when we're ready."

An hour later my friends and I had reunited with our horses, and I was leading them to Kim's office for the last part of the stable tour. I'd introduced Ana to everyone, and she fit right in. I didn't know if it was because of the Christmassy feeling in the air, but everyone was getting along. Even Taylor and Drew had zero weirdness between them. Or none that I could see, anyway.

Kim's office door was ajar and the light was on.

"Come on in," I said. "Kim won't mind."

For all of the renovations Kim *had* done, one thing that remained the same was her office. The walls were still reddish brown and covered with photos and clippings of Briar Creek's riders, past and present. Her desk was a mess of papers and files. A long shelf held dozens of trophies.

"Wow," Lexa said. She stood in front of a giant trophy—one taller than the rest. I knew who it belonged to.

Lexa brushed a cocoa-colored finger over the plaque and the inscription: SASHA SILVER.

"Sasha's trophy gave me a lot of motivation," I said. Then I giggled. "And it also intimidated me like crazy!"

At the end of the shelf, Taylor was peering closely at a photo in a silver frame. "You see this, Laur?" he asked.

I shook my head and walked over to him.

Inside the frame was a photo of *Whisper and me.* Whisper was trotting in a twenty-meter circle in Kim's arena.

"Oh my gosh," I said. "I'm on the shelf with *Sasha!*"

Everyone crowded behind me to see the photograph.

"This was the first week that I had Whisper," I said. "I didn't even know someone took this."

"Kim put that up when you left," Ana said. She pushed her wavy light-brown hair behind her shoulders. "She talks about you at lessons all the time."

I shot a look at Bri, wondering how she felt that there wasn't a trophy or photo of her on Kim's wall. But Bri's smile suggested she was okay.

"Seems like Kim's proud of *both* of her Canterwood students," Cole said, smiling.

I started to correct Cole that there were three BC-turned-Canterwood students—Sasha, me, *and* Brielle. Before I could, footsteps stopped in the doorway.

"I most certainly am."

The twelve of us turned toward the door. A blonde with her hair in its usual haphazardly-styled ponytail, clad in fawn breeches, a thick sweater, and paddock boots, smiled at us.

"Kim!" I squealed. I weaved through my friends and hugged my old instructor in the doorway. My friends and I filled up the small office, and there wasn't much more room for another body. "It's so good to see you! I missed you and Briar Creek."

"We've missed you, Lauren," Kim said, her hazel eyes warm. "I take it these are your friends. Or 'elves,' I guess."

Laughing, I nodded. "These are my friends. You might already know Bri and Ana."

Kim scrunched her nose. "Hmm. You girls don't look familiar."

Ana stuck out her tongue, and everyone laughed.

"It's great to see you, Bri," Kim said, hugging her. "Things haven't been the same since you left."

Bri raised an eyebrow, an amused look on her face. "You have to miss me bringing you a caramel macchiato from the Bean every day."

Kim grinned. "Well, yes, but classes are a bit more . . . *quiet* without you."

Bri gasped, pretending to be surprised, while the rest of us giggled.

"Kim, you remember Taylor, right?" I asked.

Taylor held up his hand from the back of the room.

"Of course. It's nice to see you again, Taylor."

I made all of the introductions, and we chatted with Kim for a few minutes.

"I want all you to make yourselves at home here," Kim said. "Please let me know if you need anything."

My eye caught on Sasha's trophy. "Do you know if Sasha's going to stop by?"

Kim blinked, then nodded. "I'm sure you'll see her around. She texted me something about coming over during break."

Excitement rippled through the room. Sasha and I weren't BFFs or anything, but we were friends. I wanted to wish her happy holidays. I crossed my fingers that we would see her.

"We're headed out to trail ride," I said to Kim. "See you later!"

A strange expression flickered across Kim's face, then vanished. It was so fast—I couldn't even be sure what I'd seen. "Have fun and be safe!" Kim told us. We emptied out of Kim's office and headed to the tack room. I couldn't wait to hit the trails!

7

DARE

Sasha

"I KNOW I KEEP SAYING IT, BUT THIS TRAIL IS beautiful, Sash," Callie said. She walked Black Jack on a loose rein beside Charm and me.

"I picked my fave one," I said. "I'm so glad you like it!"

I looked to my right at Jacob. He looked at ease on Bliss—a bay mare that Kim used for beginner riding lessons. Paige also looked comfy on a paint quarter horse—Belle—that Kim had suggested.

We were deep in the Connecticut woods, walking across a meadow. Heather and Aristocrat were near Alison and Sunstruck as they chatted. Brit and Eric were on the opposite side, walking their horses near the frozen creek.

Beneath me, Charm couldn't have been more relaxed. He seemed to remember this trail too. The open meadow often had deer grazing during the spring. A creek snaked through the meadow, and on the opposite side of the field, a stone wall with browned-from-the-cold ivy separated Kim's property from the neighbors.

"There's one super-old farmer who has property over there," I said, pointing. "He actually came to Kim's office and told her none of us were allowed to ever ride on his land." I rolled my eyes.

"Like, because the horses might ruin the crops or something?" Brit asked.

"That would be a legit reason," I said. "Except he hasn't planted anything in a zillion years! The only thing the horses would 'ruin' would be weeds."

The group laughed.

"Wouldn't he owe the riders if the horses trampled the weeds?" Alison asked. "What a nut job."

"I think we need to add a little, oh, excitement to this ride," Heather said. She met my eyes, and I saw *that* gleam in her blue eyes.

"No. No. No," I said. "No way. Did I mention 'no'?"

"Silver, come on," Heather said. "You *must* know of a way onto the property, or we could jump the wall. We could take a quick little ride and get right back to the trail."

"I can't," I said. "We all promised Kim we wouldn't, so she'd never have trouble with him."

Heather cocked her head. "This dude is old, right? Do you even see his house? I highly doubt his eyesight is good enough to spot a few horses all the way out here on the edge of his property. We won't get caught."

"I—"

"I dare you," Heather said, grinning and flashing white teeth. "All of you." She looked at each rider.

Silence. My friends' eyes shifted from Heather to me.

"Well," Callie said. "What if we jump the wall and jump right back?"

"Works for me," Heather said.

"Callie!" I turned to my friend. "What are you doing?"

"There's no way we'll get caught, Sash," Callie said. "Come on. Pleeease?"

Callie's competitive side had taken her over. She never backed down from a challenge. Especially not one from Heather.

"I'm in," Eric said. "As long as we *all* jump right back over. I don't want to get Sasha in trouble."

"Agreed," Brit said.

"I'll do it," Alison said.

All eyes were on me. Excitement at Heather's dare

pumped through me. I'd wanted to jump that wall *so* bad forever. No one would find out.

"Okay, okay!" I said.

"Yay!" Heather cheered.

I held up a finger. "One condition: Jacob and Paige stay on this side. They can't jump that wall."

The group nodded.

"Of course," Heather said. "I never said I wanted to do anything dangerous. You can be like our lookouts, Paige and Jacob."

"For birds who might go tell on you guys?" Jacob joked.

"For anyone else who might have come to the stable since we got here and decided to trail ride," I said.

"Got it covered," Paige said.

Jacob smiled at me.

I leaned closer to him, not wanting to embarrass him in front of our friends. "Are you sure you're confident enough on Bliss to be on one side of the wall while we're on the other?"

"Absolutely," Jacob said, stroking Bliss's neck. "She's a sweetheart. I feel totally safe."

"I promise the next dare will include you," I said.

Jacob grinned and winked at me.

"All right! I think Miss Fox should go first," I said.

Heather dropped her knotted reins on Aristocrat's neck and rubbed her hands together. She beamed. "I'd be honored. I'm going to canter Aristocrat in a few circles to warm him up first."

Heather tapped her heels against her gelding's side, and the chestnut broke away from the herd and moved from a trot to a smooth canter. Heather sat effortlessly to Aristocrat's smooth gait, and they made a giant, sweeping circle in the flat meadow.

"Heather knows how to turn even a trail ride into an event," Eric said, watching her.

"That she does," I said.

Heather made two more circles, then trotted Aristocrat back to the creek bed's edge. She turned Aristocrat to face the stone wall. I measured it with my eyes and guessed it was about three feet high. The ground on the other side was as flat as the meadow.

Heather gathered her reins, settled herself in the saddle, and urged Aristocrat forward. He moved into a trot, then a measured canter. His long legs ate up the ground, and soon they were strides from the wall. At the right second, Heather lifted her seat slightly out of the saddle and raised her hands along Aristocrat's neck. The liver chestnut didn't hesitate. He pushed off the ground with his hind legs, tucked his forelegs, and made a beautiful arch as he flew over the stone wall. He landed easily on the other side. That was exactly why Heather was on the Youth Equestrian National Team. Her form had been flawless. Heather let him canter a few strides before easing him into a trot and turning him back to us.

"See?" she called from the other side of the wall. "No crazy old farmer came and got me. Let's go, people!"

Now I wasn't anything but excited.

"I want to go!" I said.

Heather crooked her index finger at me. "Come to the dark side."

"Go for it," Eric said. Everyone else nodded in agreement.

I shot Jacob a smile before I squeezed my legs against Charm's sides. He was ready to go. Even though Heather and I were friends now, I don't think Charm had ever gotten over his rivalry with Aristocrat. He'd watched the other horse jump, and I knew Charm—he wanted to do better.

"We've got to warm you up," I whispered to Charm. Talking to Charm while I rode him was one habit of mine that Mr. Conner hadn't been able to break. I felt more connected when I talked to my mounts.

I took a deep breath of cold air as I let out the reins a bit and let Charm move from a trot to a canter. He jumped into a canter in a stride and I guided him in a large circle. He yanked his head up, swishing his tail. He wanted more rein to go faster. I tightened my fingers on the reins and pressed my tailbone into the saddle. We were going fast enough. I wasn't about to let him fly over a stone wall—an object that wouldn't move if Charm took a misstep and hit it.

Charm's ears flicked back and forth. He wasn't happy that I didn't let him go faster, but I stayed firm and didn't give in. We completed another circle, and then I pointed him in the direction of the forbidden wall. The second Charm realized we were about to jump, his tail swished excitedly and he put his attention on me. His hoofbeats pounded on the brown grass as we neared the wall.

At the right second, I moved into a two-point position and took my weight off Charm's back. Charm thrust into the air and snapped his front legs under his body. I loved the feeling of being airborne. The landing was easy, and I let Charm canter a few strides and patted his neck. Grinning, I turned him back to face Heather and Aristocrat on our side of the wall and the rest of my friends on the other.

"That was the *best!*" I called.

That's when I noticed Jacob jerking his head in the direction of the entrance to the meadow. That's when I noticed none of my friends were looking at me, but instead toward the middle of the meadow. That's when I noticed a dozen horses and riders making their way toward us.

8

TRÈS UNEXPECTED TRAILMATES

Lauren

"WHAT SHOULD WE DO?" I WHISPERED TO everyone. "They've already seen us! We'd look dumb just turning around, right?"

"Why would we go back?" Zack asked. He held Nero's reins in one hand as the liver chestnut gelding walked beside Scout, Garret's mount.

"Because I can't see who they are, and we probably don't know them," I said.

"Plus," Ana said, angling Breeze, her strawberry roan mare, closer, "they're totally breaking Briar Creek's rules. We *all* know we're not allowed to jump the wall and ride on the neighbor's land. He's some insane farmer who would probably have those riders arrested for trespassing."

Cole pulled Valentino, his black gelding, beside me.

"We should say hi. We're not the ones doing anything wrong. Why cut our ride short?"

I looked at Drew. I needed his opinion. He always knew what to do.

"I agree with Cole," Drew said. "Let's ride past them and just be casual."

Whisper tugged at the reins, seeing the other horses and wanting to get closer. I kept her at a slow walk.

"Okay," I said, nodding. "You guys are right—we're not done riding, and there's still more trail to see."

Our group moved at a faster walk across the meadow. I squinted at the other riders and horses, but they were still too far away. None of them moved—the two horses and riders on the wrong side of the property stayed there, and the rest of the riders waited on our side of the wall.

"Lauren," Khloe said. "Omigod. On the other side of the wall. Is that—?"

"Sasha Silver!" I said, cutting her off. "No way! Those are her friends from Canterwood!"

I'm going to kill Kim, I thought. *She knew all along that I was going to run into Sasha out on the trails.* Knowing Kim, if she hadn't said anything to us, then Sasha was in the dark, too, to keep things fair.

I spotted someone I thought was Callie Harper, and

a girl who looked like Heather Fox on the other side of the wall with Sasha. Sasha was the *parfait* model student at Canterwood. I'd never heard about her getting into trouble. Maybe I didn't know as much about Sasha as I thought.

I lifted my hand in a friendly wave, and Sasha glanced at Heather, then waved back. She looked comfy but chic in fawn breeches, boots, a black helmet, and a coat. She motioned for us to come over.

"I think I'm going to faint," Lexa said in a whisper. She slowed Honor, her mare. "I've never met Sasha Silver!"

"I don't know if I'm ready for this!" Khloe added. "It's like meeting a celebrity." She squared her shoulders, dropped her heels, smoothed Ever's black mane, and tucked in her elbows. Quickly, the rest of my group fixed their riding posture too.

"Lauren!" Sasha called. "Hi!"

"Hey!" I said. I drew Whisper to a halt as we reached her friends.

"What are you doing here?" Sasha and I asked each other at the same time.

Everyone laughed—kind of an uneasy laugh. I was glad I wasn't the only one who didn't know what to do in this situation.

"I came home for Christmas and brought my friends with me," I said. I introduced everyone. Clare choked out a "Hello" and stared with wide eyes at Sasha.

"What about you?" I asked Sasha.

"Same as you," the older girl said. "I'm with my parents for the holidays, and I convinced my besties to come along."

"This is so insane," I said. "We're *all* here, and you guys have your horses too."

"Who wants to spend the holidays without their horse?" Sasha asked, smiling.

"So, Lauren," Heather said. "You're not going to gallop back to the stable and tell on us, are you?"

I gulped. Heather made me nervous. I remembered Sasha telling me that she and Heather weren't enemies any longer, but Heather had done something to become an arch-nemesis of Sasha's. I was going to be extra careful around her.

"Um, no, of course not," I sputtered. I wanted all of Sasha's friends to like me, and I didn't want any of them to think I was a tattletale.

"*Um*," Heather said, her tone mimicking mine. "Are you sure?"

I was glad there was a wall separating us. The girl was scary!

"I'm not saying anything," I said. I lifted my chin and locked eyes with Heather.

"Heather, chill," Sasha said, shooting her friend a look.

"What are you guys doing?" Khloe asked. I was glad there was someone else other than me talking from our group.

"We were trail riding," Sasha said. "But Heather gets bored kind of easily. She dared all of us to jump the wall onto the neighbor's land."

"The crazy, grumpy farmer?" I asked. I almost said, *Aren't you scared?!* but I didn't want to seem like a baby.

Sasha nodded. "Yeah. We know we're not supposed to be here, but we're jumping right back over."

"I'm the lookout," a guy, Jacob, said. "I've only ridden a couple of times and never jumped, so I got out of this dare."

"I'm not really a rider either," Taylor said. The two guys exchanged understanding looks. Despite Tay's lack of experience, I doubted anyone would have been able to tell from the way he sat astride Zombie—a gray gelding of Kim's.

A redhead, Paige Parker, I think, raised her hand. "I'm on lookout duty too."

I was glad for Taylor that there were other new-slash-not-really-riders among us.

"You guys said 'dare,'" Clare said. She'd edged Fuego, her fire-colored chestnut gelding, closer to Sasha's crew. "Who's next?"

Heather exchanged a look across the wall with Alison Robb—a willowy girl. Alison was on a beautiful palomino Arabian. The gelding's face was delicate, and he had a gorgeous dished nose.

"How about you?" Heather said to Clare.

I shot a look at Clare. *Wait a second!* I wanted to say. This was Sasha and her friends' thing. My group and I were staying out of trouble and were having plenty of fun trail riding—on the right side of the wall.

Clare's hesitation was palpable. Her face blushed almost the same color as her hair. I wanted to jump in and answer "No, thanks" for her. But I didn't want to look like a chicken in front of Sasha and her friends.

"Heather, stop," Sasha said, glaring at her friend. "Leave Lauren and her friends alone."

I said a silent thank-you to Sasha. Whew. That settled it, and now we could leave Sasha's group alone to their dare and keep going on our trail ride.

Clare straightened in the saddle and looked at Heather. "You're on." She turned Fuego away from the wall and broke apart from our group.

I wheeled Whisper around and rode next to Clare. "What are you doing?" I hissed. "It's a *huge* rule not to ride on the neighbor's land. What if Kim finds out and we get kicked out of Briar Creek for the rest of break?"

Nero, Zack's liver chestnut gelding, snorted as if he understood me and was offering his opinion.

"We won't," Clare said. "Laur, it's *Sasha*. I can't say no to jumping in front of her and the rest of her friends. I'll jump the stone wall, turn around, and come right back over. I promise."

"I completely understand you wanting to impress Sasha," I said. "I feel the same way. But she doesn't care if you say no to a dare. You'll have a chance at Canterwood for her to see you ride sometime—I know it."

Clare's big blue eyes looked into mine. "Please don't be mad about this. I won't get us in trouble."

I pulled Whisper to a halt, sighing. "Okay," I said with a small smile. "Just hurry back over. Go kill it."

I circled Whisper back to face my friends and Sasha and her group. "We're not going to get in trouble," I said to my friends. "If anyone else wants to join in, go for it."

Khloe, who was beside Zack and Nero, walked Ever next to Whisper and me. The bay mare and Whisper sniffed each other's muzzles. Subtly, Khloe tilted her head toward the other side of the meadow. We let the horses amble away from the group, making it look as though we were keeping them warmed up.

"You sure you're okay with this?" Khloe said in a whisper. "I know you don't want to potentially make Kim mad."

"I didn't like it at first," I admitted. "I don't want to break Kim's rules and disrespect her. *But* no one's hurting anyone and there's no one else here. We'll be back to the stables before we know it."

Khloe nodded. "I'm glad you feel okay. I know you would have said no if you had felt uncomfortable. You're not really an easy mark for peer pressure, no matter how piercing blue the eyes are of the girl offering the dare."

I laughed. "Right?! I'm glad it's not just me."

We turned the horses around and rejoined the group.

Across the field, Clare cantered Fuego in an even circle, then slowed him to a trot. She walked him close to the creek bed before turning him to face the wall.

"Go, Clare!" Khloe cheered.

"Shhh!" at least four people from Sasha's group said simultaneously.

"Sorry," Khloe said in a whisper. She made an *oops* face at me.

Clare moved Fuego into a trot, and after a few strides,

he moved into a canter. Clare's royal-blue jacket contrasted sharply against Fuego's red coat. The pair moved toward the wall, and I crossed my fingers for Clare. She was a great jumper, and now I was glad she'd accepted Heather's challenge. She was representing us, and I knew she was going to do it well!

All of our heads turned to watch as Clare and Fuego swept by us and reached the wall. Clare lifted out of the saddle, hands sliding along Fuego's neck, and he pushed off the ground. He rose over the stones with inches to spare and landed lightly on the other side. I wanted to cheer as Khloe had done, but I didn't want to draw attention to what we were doing. Maybe the farmer had supersonic hearing or something.

A grinning Clare turned Fuego back to face all of us. Now she was one of the three on the other side of the wall. Quickly, she wiped the grin off her face and replaced it with a look of nonchalance. Like it was every day that she jumped a stone wall at a strange stable onto forbidden property.

"Niiice!" Sasha said to Clare. She put up a palm for a high five.

Clare couldn't stop her smile this time. Beaming, she slapped Sasha's palm and stroked Fuego's neck.

Heather merely nodded at her before turning her gaze back to the fourteen of us on the other side. "Next person better get over here," Heather said. As if to back up her words, her liver chestnut struck the ground with a foreleg. "I don't want to be waiting until New Year's."

Without a word, Callie turned her gelding, cantered in two circles, then cleared the wall.

One by one, the rest of us jumped the wall. Cole, Khloe, Alison, Drew, Garret, Carina, Brit, Ana, me, Brielle, Zack, Eric, and Lexa.

Taylor, Paige, and Jacob were left on the opposite side of the wall. They'd sidled their horses next to each other and had been chatting while we jumped. I'd caught a few words like "PlayStation" and "Nintendo." Paige had a look of "Boys!" on her face.

"I declare this dare complete," Heather addressed us. She raised an eyebrow as she looked at me and my friends. "It was a surprise to have you join us and not bail, kids."

"It was fun. We're the kind of 'kids' who don't back down," Khloe shot back.

Alpha female against alpha female. Both blond girls eyed each other—neither breaking contact.

Finally Heather nodded. "Maybe we'll see you on the trails again while we're here."

Sasha's lips curved into a small smile. I wanted to dance in my saddle. We—the lowly just-turned seventh graders—had gotten an invitation from Heather Fox to ride with her. Heather was practically as big a deal on campus as Sasha. This was *huge*!

"You should def text me when you're coming over to ride," Sasha said, looking at me. "We'll join you if we're free."

"Cool. I will," I said.

"Let's get back on our turf before anything happens," Sasha said.

With that, we each took turns jumping our horses over the wall. I didn't let out a full breath of relief until each and every one of us was back on Kim's land. If this was what trail riding with Heather was like, something told me that I'd better prepare myself.

9

PUT ON YOUR
ELF SUITS!

Sasha

IT WAS STILL DARK OUTSIDE WHEN MY ALARM clock buzzed the next morning. It was six and time to get up and get ready to go to the first day at Safe Haven for Thoroughbreds. It didn't even feel like a Monday, usually my least fave day of the week, since it was break.

Callie rubbed her eyes, sitting up and smiling sleepily from the daybed. "I can't wait to get to the rescue center," she said.

"Me either. This is going to be the super-best Christmas break *ever*," I said. "We've got all of our friends, our horses, and we're helping new horses find homes." *Like, one could come home with me,* I thought. I'd dropped a few not-so-subtle hints to Mom and Dad that it would be giving back to the community if *I* adopted a horse from

Safe Haven. But they'd said that I was doing more than enough by volunteering.

"It's a twenty-four-seven horse fest," Callie said. She got up and picked breeches and a yellow thermal shirt from her suitcase. "Speaking of horses, I was kind of caught off guard by Lauren Towers and her friends yesterday."

It felt like old times between Callie and me. We were about to have a gossip fest, and it was like none of the baggage we had from the past existed. Maybe the holiday spirit helped wipe it all away.

"I was surprised to see Lauren too," I said. "More shocked, though, that she had all of her friends there. She planned a Christmas like ours."

"I figured we would probably run into her sometime at Briar Creek," Callie said. "It was weird, though."

"Why?" I pulled a hunter-green wool sweater over my head. After our ride, Kim had explained to all of us that she'd kept quiet about each of our groups coming to BC because she'd wanted us to feel out the sitch ourselves.

Callie shrugged. "It was almost like she was ready to compete with us or something. She and her friends didn't hesitate at Heather's dare. I mean, I'm glad they did it, because I got to see for myself that the rumors about them are true."

"What rumors?"

"That they're gunning for spots on their advanced team as soon as they have tryouts. That girl, Khloe, who's already on the advanced team, is YENT material."

Callie and I both slid our feet into thick socks and started lacing up our boots.

"They're not our competition," I said. "Lauren and her friends are a grade behind us. We don't have to worry about our slots on the advanced team and the YENT."

"You sure?" Callie asked. "Tell me that you don't think Mr. Conner might combine our advanced team with theirs for a practice every once in a while. Or offer them a chance to try out for the YENT sooner than our chances."

I shook my head. "That would never happen. Mr. Conner keeps every grade separate. He'd never let them jump ahead in line, either, no matter how good they are."

I finished tying my laces, my mind racing from what Callie had said. Lauren's background was better than mine. She had a champion pedigree before I had even completed my first double oxer. I swallowed. Next semester wouldn't bring *that* kind of change to Canterwood . . . would it?

Callie stood, helmet in hand. "Ready?"

"Yeah," I said. "Let's go gather everybody and grab

some breakfast. No more thinking or talking about Lauren until we see her again. Deal?"

Callie smiled. "Deal."

We left my room, and the boys' door was already open. The smell of bacon, eggs, and sausage lingered in the air.

Callie and I walked into the kitchen and found Paige at the stove, flitting between pots and pans like a hummingbird.

"Morning!" Paige said, smiling. She was dressed in a pair of my boots and breeches. "Sash, I told your mom that I'd love to cook breakfast for everyone. I wanted to do something since she's letting us stay here."

I grinned. "My parents will never let you leave," I said. "Not once they've tasted Chef Parker's cooking."

With a flick of her wrist and a satisfied smile, Paige flipped a perf omelet onto a plate in front of me.

10

DO YOU SEE WHAT I SEE?

Lauren

"WELCOME, EVERYONE!"

My friends and I stood in a warm indoor arena at Safe Haven for Thoroughbreds. I eyed the fifteen or so other volunteers with us—most of them looking like they were in college or older. We had gathered around the volunteer director as she stood on a mounting block to address us.

"I'm Lyssa, a name you might recognize from e-mails from our group," the petite brunette said. "I can't thank you all enough for being here this morning *and* for the time you have offered to dedicate to some very deserving horses."

Taylor and I exchanged excited smiles. We'd all gotten here early this morning and signed in—wanting to make a good impression on our first day. The rest of my friends surrounded us and directed their attention to Lyssa.

"As many of you know, life for ex-racehorses can be extremely challenging," Lyssa said. "For some, their life begins and ends with the track. I want to make it clear that I am not here to advocate against the sport of horse racing—only to inform you about the reality of what happens to some, not all, ex-racehorses."

From somewhere in the stable, a whinny from one horse set off a chorus of neighs.

Lyssa smiled. "I'm an ex-jockey. I started racing in high school and rode for many years. My career ended about five years ago due to an injury. I knew nothing else but racing. What was I supposed to do with my life? That's kind of what it's like for some of our horses."

"It's *so* cool that she used to be a jockey," Ana whispered to me.

I nodded. "She got hurt and she's *still* involved with horses. That's awesome."

"Some racehorses suffer injuries during their careers and are put down by their owners," Lyssa said. "Not all earn enough money from races to make valuable studs or broodmares. Those that aren't put down are sometimes sent to the auction block to be sold and retrained for various uses. Others are sold for practically pennies to slaughterhouses."

My stomach turned. I couldn't even think about or really try to process Lyssa's last sentence. It wasn't something that I didn't already know, but hearing it was different. Maybe the fact that we were surrounded by horses made it harder to think about too.

"Safe Haven, like many similar groups, is a nonprofit organization that rescues ex-racehorses who are in danger of being euthanized. Sadly, we cannot save every horse. Even some that we do rescue have to be put down because their injuries are so severe. We don't want to keep a horse alive if there's no chance of recovering and if the quality of life is not pleasant for that animal."

Lyssa shifted on the block. She looked down, almost as if composing herself, then glanced back up at us.

"But for the horses we save," Lyssa said, a smile on her face, "we are lucky enough to get to know them, care for them, and rehabilitate them for a new life. Their new purpose could vary from a light pleasure horse, to a stable horse for lessons, a therapy horse used for children and adults with disabilities, or a companion that cannot be ridden but *can* be loved by an adopter."

Lyssa nodded at an older girl who had her hand raised.

"Are all the horses up for adoption?" the girl asked.

"No," Lyssa said. "Some horses have been through too

much trauma for us to feel comfortable placing them in a new home. Some of the horses who are up for adoption have been with us for months or years and haven't found the right match yet."

I frowned. It made me sad to think of a horse waiting to be chosen for a new home.

"We do not euthanize those horses," Lyssa continued. "Through donations, we are able to provide them with a place to live out the rest of their natural lives."

Mom and Dad were in trouble. Now I wanted to adopt a stable full of ex-racehorses! Somehow, I didn't think that was a Christmas present they would go for. I thought back to my birthday party, when I'd asked for donations to SHT. It wasn't the same as actually adopting a horse, but raising money to help the cause was something I was going to keep doing.

"The details of jobs we need completed are listed in the information packet that I'll pass out now," Lyssa said. "Please make sure everyone gets one, and read through the entire packet. Many of you signed up with friends, and the coordinators did their best to keep those groups together during specific time slots. The times and days we're expecting you vary. If you have more time to spare, you're obviously more than welcome to come whenever you'd like."

A stack of packets reached me. I took one of the thick packets and handed the rest to Brielle. She did the same and passed it to Zack, who was shoulder to shoulder with Khloe. The two weren't officially boyfriend and girlfriend, but they had been on enough dates that I bet Zack was going to ask KK the big question soon. They complemented each other perfectly. Zack was funny and animated like Khloe. He was also *très* cute, with dark-blond hair—something Khloe especially liked.

"Each task is labeled with the required experience needed from you," Lyssa said. "For example, you'll see on page five that 'Advertising' has a label of 'No experience.' The task of 'Exercising' has a label of 'Advanced' beside it. Each task is color coordinated to match the name tag you should have picked up when you signed in this morning."

I looked down at the laminated card that hung from my neck. My name was highlighted in green. Advanced tasks were green. All of my friends' tags matched mine in color. Taylor's name on his tag was in red—no experience. I wondered if he felt uncomfortable with a red tag, but as I looked around the crowd, I saw more red tags than I'd expected. Hopefully, that would make Tay feel like he fit in.

"There are lockers for you to store water bottles,

snacks—whatever you'd like," Lyssa said. "You'll find the lockers just outside the arena near the tack room. Since it's the first day, your only task today was to attend orientation. Since I'm not here all of the time, there are different coordinators to help steer you in the right direction."

"How do we know who's a coordinator?" a guy from the other side of the crowd asked.

"All coordinators' names are typed in bold font and have a star next to them," Lyssa said.

I spotted a starred badge a few people away. *If I volunteer here every holiday and each summer, I wonder if I could be a coordinator?* I thought.

"If you'd like to stay," Lyssa continued, "please feel free to do so. You're welcome to watch some of our regular volunteers and get a feel for what you may be doing during your time with us."

Lyssa smiled and clasped her hands in front of her. "Thank you all for your time during the holiday season. We wouldn't be able to hold our annual adopt-a-thon without people like you. I'll be here if anyone has questions, and please come ready to work when your first shift arrives. You'll find the name of your coordinator next to your time slot. Again, thank you, and I can't wait to get started!"

The arena filled with applause. I clapped so hard, my hands stung. With a little wave, Lyssa stepped off the mounting block. I turned to my friends.

"Is this the coolest thing or what?" I asked.

"I'm *so* excited!" Cole said. His green eyes were wide and almost the same color as the highlighted text on his name tag.

Garret flipped through the packet. "Are we all in the same group?"

I flipped a few pages and stopped.

"Yep!" Clare said. "There are all of our names. We're on Tuesday afternoon. Score!"

"Uh . . . ," Khloe started, an odd look on her face. "Do you guys see—"

"No way!" I said. I peered at my paper. I was having a hallucination. I mean, I've never had one before, but this had to be one. I blinked. But the words were there in black ink, not disappearing no matter how many times I blinked.

"Looks like we have company," Drew said, his voice low.

I looked at him, expecting him to be staring at the paper too, but he was gazing over my shoulder.

"Are you stalking us?" Sasha asked as I turned around to face her. Her smile assured me she was kidding.

"Totally," I teased back. "We not only chose the same

place to volunteer, *but* we also made sure we got almost every time slot that you guys did."

The other Canterwood students stopped next to us. Most of them smiled at my comment. I realized that Sasha and I were the two who stood slightly in front of the rest of our friends. *She* was the leader of the legendary Sasha & Co., but I certainly wasn't a "leader" of my group. I took a tiny step back so I was aligned with Drew.

"I can't believe you're all here too," Sasha said. "Lauren, was this how you convinced your parents to let you bring friends home for Christmas?"

"Actually, yes," I said. "And our horses, too."

"We should all wear matching Canterwood Crest sweatshirts every day," Paige said.

"Ooh, yeah!" Callie said with a giggle as she high-fived Paige. "We *are* representing Canterwood."

Everyone laughed.

"Speaking of school," Garret said, adjusting the black beanie over his red hair, "I'm sure Headmistress Drake has spies here *somewhere* making sure we don't"—he paused—"'tarnish the reputation of an elite institution.'"

Everybody laughed.

"That's *exactly* what Headmistress Drake would say," Eric said. "Your impression was dead-on too."

The dark-haired guy smiled at Garret. I'd heard stories that Sasha, who was now dating Jacob, had dated Eric. *Does every guy who meets Sasha ask her out?* I thought.

"The headmistress probably had cameras installed in the stable," Brit Chan said. The pretty girl had her long black hair in a low side braid. I knew that she was Sasha's roommate at school.

I realized both of our groups had melded into a cluster as we bantered back and forth.

"That's not enough," Lexa said. Her big brown eyes were wide. "I bet there are tiny cameras hidden somewhere on the tack so she can monitor us when we're exercising the horses."

Heather gave Lexa a quick grin. "Not bad. I was thinking the same thing."

I could almost feel Lexa's excitement from Heather's compliment.

"I'm glad you guys were here," Sasha said. "We were ready on time, but my dad overslept."

"You probably want to sign in," I said. "You'll get a name badge like this." I held mine up. "Lyssa, the volunteer director, has info packets. She's . . ." I looked for her and finally spotted the woman, surrounded by volunteers. I pointed. ". . . the one being swarmed by people."

Taylor held out his info packet to Jacob. "You want to keep that and make copies for you guys? It would probably take you longer to get to Lyssa."

Jacob, smiling, took the papers. "Thanks. Taylor, right? Sorry—I'm bad with names."

Taylor nodded. "You can keep mine. I'll share with one of my friends."

"Thank you," Sasha said. "I really didn't want to have to go up to Lyssa and have our first impression be that we're the ones who missed orientation."

"Lyssa's really nice," I said. "I don't think she'd hold anything against you. Nothing she said was info that's not in the packet."

"Thanks for the heads-up," Jacob said. "And if Drake's watching us, we better stop standing around talking."

Sasha smiled at Jacob, slipping her hand into his. "Good point. Let's go sign in, guys."

We traded "See you laters," and my group hung back as Sasha and her friends left the arena to sign in.

I turned to my friends. "I don't know about you guys, but it feels like it would be kind of a waste of time to call my dad to come get us. We really just got here. What do you think?"

"I agree," Ana said. "I really want to look around."

Garret nodded. "Me too."

"Okay!" Khloe said, bouncing on her toes. "Girl time!"

"Girl time?" Zack asked, shaking his head. "Am I supposed to know what that means?"

Khloe lightly smacked Zack's upper arm. "It means you *guys* are going to go do whatever boys do for a while so the *girls* can talk." She smiled sweetly at Zack.

"You were together all night and this morning," Cole said. "There's still more to talk about?"

"Um, *always!*" Clare said. She shook her head, and the rest of us joined in with pretend disgusted looks at the boys.

"Guys, meet us at the stable entrance in an hour?" Lexa asked.

With nods of agreement, we split up.

11

ALL I WANT FOR CHRISTMAS IS YOU

Lauren

"AHHH!" KHLOE SAID, GRABBING MY ARM. She had the famous Khloe look—like she had to talk or she would burst. "I was *dying* to talk to you guys, but I couldn't say what I wanted to in front of the boys."

Carina giggled. "Dying, huh? I had an idea that something was going on when you looked at me and kept blinking—like you were trying to send me a message in Morse code or something."

Khloe nodded, her blond hair flying. "I was! Well, not in Morse code because I don't know how, but I was trying to tell you that we needed girl time. I couldn't say anything especially because of Zack."

We wandered out of the arena and into a side yard. People and horses were everywhere. Volunteers were leading Thoroughbreds to and from the stable, catching and releasing them into paddocks, or grooming horses standing at tie rings. At least a dozen riders were exercising horses.

"Let's go sit on the fence and watch the horses being exercised in that arena," Brielle said. She tipped her chin toward a giant rectangle-shaped arena not too far away. "The boys aren't there, and neither are Sasha and her friends."

We walked to the arena, climbed the wooden fence, and settled ourselves on the top rail. I sat next to Khloe, with Ana on my other side. Four horses worked in the arena. A gray that reminded me of Whisper trotted in large circles in front of us. Two bays walked along the fence at the opposite end of the arena. In the center, a chestnut gelding fought his rider. The rider, an athletic-looking girl in a black wool coat, white helmet with visible scrapes, and worn-in paddock boots, struggled to hold the horse at a trot. The chestnut tossed his head and crow hopped, yanking the reins in the girl's hands. The girl's attention never wavered. The horse's antics had captured the attention of all of us—no one said a word as we watched.

The rider, who looked about Charlotte's age, refused to give in to the horse. She pushed her heels down and sat deep in the saddle. The gelding tossed his head again, seesawing the reins against his neck.

"Think we'll get any horses like that to exercise?" Carina said quietly.

"I don't know," I said. "Maybe only the volunteers who have been here for a long time get the really green horses. Or maybe our experience levels will be enough for us to be assigned a horse that isn't quiet to work with."

I hoped I'd get to ride a horse that needed some retraining. It would be a challenge and something that I could learn from. Khloe's knee bumped into mine, and I remembered why we had chosen to separate ourselves from the guys.

"Spill," I said, elbowing Khloe lightly. Each girl sitting on the fence turned her gaze from the unruly chestnut to Khloe.

"I couldn't wait until we got back to your place, Laur, to talk about Sasha and Co.," Khlo said, using the group's nickname.

"Omigod! So crazy, right?!" Clare said.

"Seriously!" Ana added, shaking her head. "What are the odds that *Sasha Silver* ended up volunteering here too?"

"It really is like Sasha and her friends planned the same Christmas vacay we did," I said. "We'll probably see them again at Briar Creek, we know we'll see them here, and Union isn't very big. If we go out for dinner or grab coffee in the morning, we could run into them."

"We, like, *never* see them at school, but we've run into Sasha so many times already since we've been in Union," Bri said. "So weird."

The other girls nodded. Hoofbeats approached us, and we fell silent as a tall, lanky bay walked past us. I didn't want to talk until the horse was out of earshot, in case my voice spooked him.

"I'm *so* lucky to be dating Zack," Khloe said once the bay and his rider were a safe distance away from us. "And no guy is cuter than him, but I have to say it: Sasha's ex and her current BF are *so* cute!"

We giggled and nodded.

"I feel the same way about Drew," I said. "But I agree with you, KK. Sasha's so lucky! Jacob and Eric are the hottest guys in her grade. Does anyone know why Sasha and Eric broke up?"

I looked at Khloe, Clare, and Lexa, since they'd been at Canterwood longer than Brielle, Carina, and me.

The three girls shook their heads.

"I heard rumors," Clare said. She brushed a red lock of hair out of her blue eyes. "Somebody in my art class told me that Sasha dated Jacob first, and then they broke up and she went out with Eric. Then *they* split, and Sasha went back to Jacob."

Lexa nodded, leaning forward so I could see her from her spot farthest from me. "Jacob's supposedly Sasha's first love. It's so romantic! Like a movie. I heard Sasha and Eric were really great together, but Jacob was always 'the one.'" A dreamy smile came over Lexa's face. "They were meant to be together."

I sighed, loving Lexa's story, and Ana made the same noise. I bumped my shoulder against hers and we both laughed.

"I don't even go to Canterwood, but now I want to just for the gossip and stories like this!" Ana said. She played with the ends of her light-brown hair. "If I went, though, Jeremy would have to come with me."

"Oh, Ana-Banana," I said. "Remember the days when you were Miss Anti-Romance and all about your artwork?"

Ana shrugged. "I have no idea what you're talking about, Lauren. You must be thinking of someone else."

"Funny," Bri said, tilting her head. "I seem to have the same memories that LT does. There was an Ana who swore off boys until this totally hot guy came up to her at the end-of-year dance."

"Please keep talking about this cute guy," Lexa said. "This is a good story!"

Ana, Brielle, and I laughed. It felt like old times—the three of us together and having fun.

"There were two best friends who practically *dragged* this girl to the dance," I said. "Shocker—not—when the girl was asked to dance by one of the cuties, that made a lot of other girls crazy jealous."

Ana, smiling, hung her head then lifted it. "You two are starting to jog my memory a little. This girl—who's supposedly me—was maybe uninterested in boys. Or maybe the right guy hadn't appeared until the dance."

"Aww!" Carina said. "I'm guessing this guy is Jeremy, right? The one you would want to come with you to Canterwood?"

Ana did a little dance on the fence. "Okay, okay! You broke me." She laughed. "Yes, the guy who asked me to dance was Jeremy. We've been dating ever since."

"C'mon," I said. "You can be more specific than that. How long exactly?"

"Seven months, two weeks, and one day!" Ana answered immediately.

Everyone laughed, including Ana.

"You're so lucky," Carina said. "You've got a boyfriend,

Lauren has Drew, and Khloe's with Zack. I've never had a BF before."

"Welcome to the club," Lexa said. She extended a hand to Carina, and they shook hands.

"Maybe we should wish for boys to appear under the Christmas tree this year," Clare said.

"Not the tree," Khloe said. "Wish for under the mistletoe!"

We stayed on the fence, laughing quietly and chatting about boys. My mind drifted to Brielle's own boy-related past: a string of one-time dates at Yates Prepatory followed by a few dates with her longtime crush, Will, and finally, Brielle and Taylor. I waited to feel anger in the pit of my stomach about Bri's betrayal, but it didn't come. Instead, I kept giggling and talking with my friends, not one thought of Brielle and Taylor together coming to mind and dimming my happy mood.

12

NAUGHTY
OR NICE?

Sasha

"I COULDN'T THINK OF A BETTER WAY TO END the day," Brit said. She looked supercute in lounge-y clothes—a hot-pink velour tracksuit with a long-sleeve white tee that said WHERE'S THE MISTLETOE? in rhinestones.

"Totally agree," I said. "If you grab that tray, I've got this one."

"Got it." Brit picked up the green-and-red tray full of snacks. We had Chex Mix and bowls of caramel, cheese, and butter popcorn.

Brit and I had finished filling bowls with munchies for everyone. Paige, Eric, and Alison had already carried steaming mugs of hot chocolate into the other room.

We'd all agreed to do our own thing once we had gotten back to my house around lunchtime. Each of us had taken quick showers and changed out of our stable clothes. Mom had grilled cheese sandwiches for us and we'd chowed down. Eventually, we'd all wound up chatting in the den. I'd been flopped on the couch reading celeb gossip on my BlackBerry. Then Heather and Alison had joined me. We'd gotten into a long talk about how amazing all of the horses were and how much we wished we could take all of them home with us. Mid-convo, the rest of my friends had wandered into the den.

"What're you guys up to, hon?" I looked up, almost bumping into my dad.

I motioned to the tray in my hand. "We're having snacks and hot chocolate in the den." I smiled and sidestepped him, with Brit behind me.

I entered the den, passed the tray to Jacob, and surveyed the space.

Everyone was sprawled on the floor. The Christmas tree lights were on—the only light needed in the room—and the colored bulbs cast a soft light over everything. A fire crackled in the fireplace, and there were enough throw blankets for everyone.

I sat next to Jacob, our backs resting against the couch. Across from us, Heather and Alison shared a fleece throw.

"This popcorn is delish," Paige said. "Thanks, Sash."

Dad walked in, stopping in the middle of our ragged circle. "Is there enough light on in here?" he asked. "I can't see a thing. Can you all see?"

I looked at everyone. They all nodded at Dad. "We're good, Dad," I said. "I can turn on a light if we need it."

"Okay," Dad said. He put his hands in the pockets of his gray sweatpants and left the den.

"Sorry, Paige," I said. "The popcorn totally came from the store. You know what happens if I even try to make regular microwave popcorn."

Paige giggled and everyone else joined in.

"Sasha set the microwave on fire," Paige said through her giggles. "She didn't press the popcorn button and just guessed on the timer."

Footsteps shuffled down the two steps into our sunken den, and, still laughing, I looked up to see Dad.

Again.

"Sorry," Dad said. He held his reading glasses in one hand. "I forgot my book."

We all munched on food while Dad walked to one of the recliners near the fireplace. He shuffled through a few books, took one, and finally left.

I shook my head. "Sorry again," I said, whispering. I

didn't want to hurt Dad's feelings if he was close enough to hear. "He's being weird. I have no clue why."

"Back to the story," Callie said. She stretched out on her stomach and rested her chin on her hands. "I need to hear the end of this popcorn saga!"

"Yes!" Alison said. "How long did you set the timer for?"

I sniffed, raising my chin in the air. "I don't know. As long as popcorn *should* take. Like fifteen minutes."

That caused another round of laughter.

"I bet that nearly made Livvie combust," Eric said.

I nodded, thinking of my dorm hall monitor when I'd lived in Winchester. "Yeeeaaaah. She might have banned me from the microwave."

Jacob put his arm around me and kissed my cheek. "Thankfully, I'm not dating you for your cooking skills."

"You'd starve," I said. "And—"

Dad walked past us and peered hard at the fireplace mantel.

"Dad?" I asked. "What are you doing? If you forgot something else, do I need to start worrying about your memory loss?"

My dad ran a hand over his light-brown hair, shaking his head. "You have a few more years before it's time to worry about that. I'm just . . ."

Dad trailed off as he kept looking at the mantel. Slowly, I felt Jacob's arm shift until it was back at his side. I frowned, looking at him. He shifted his green eyes between us and then at my dad. *What?* I mouthed. Jacob did the same gesture.

"Oh!" I said aloud.

Everyone turned their head to me, including my dad.

"Sorry," I said. "Totally did not mean to say that out loud. I was just thinking about tomorrow."

Dad picked up the set of glass reindeer on the mantel, examined them, and put them down.

"Dad?" I asked. "Can I help you find something?"

"No, no," Dad said. "You kids go right ahead and keep having fun. Pretend I'm not even here."

Um, impossible.

"Hey, Eric," Jacob said. "Want to see this new phone app I got today?"

Eric paused for a half second, flicking his eyes to my dad and then Jacob. "Yeah, definitely."

Jacob got up from beside me, walked over to where Eric sat against a recliner, and pulled up who knows what on his phone. Now the guys were semi-separated from the girls.

"Ah," Dad said. "I think I'm looking for a decoration

that your mom turned into an ornament. Let me check this tree, then I'll be out of here."

I wanted to throw popcorn at Dad! He was *seriously* going to go through every ornament on our tree until he found the one he was "looking" for?

I leaned over to Heather. "I'm going to talk to my mom," I said in a whisper. "Be right back."

"Going to invite her to join the search party?" Heather whispered back. She smirked as I stood up. I grabbed a throw pillow from the couch and lightly bonked the top of her head.

"Silver! Dead!" Heather whisper-shouted at me.

I grinned, my back to her as I hurried out of the den. I turned down the hallway and almost jogged to my parents' room.

"Mom," I said the second I reached the doorway.

"Are you okay, honey?" Mom asked. She waved a hand at me, motioning for me to come inside. She was lying in bed under a knitted red blanket with her feet peeking out. Her golden-brown hair, the same color as mine, was loose around her shoulders. She was in yoga pants, a Canterwood sweatshirt washed so many times the colors had faded, and her fave holiday socks—woolly white ones with red-and-green reindeer.

"Dad has to be stopped," I said. I stood at the foot of the bed. "He kept coming into the den, and I thought he really just forgot something or was making sure we were all comfortable. But then I realized—it's because of Eric and Jacob! Dad's freaking out that I'm hanging in the 'dark' den with boys."

Mom laughed quietly and shook her head. "Your father told me that he was making us tea. I've had this holiday movie on Hallmark paused for fifteen minutes waiting for him. Let me go drag him in here and tell him to leave you and your friends alone."

"Thank you, Mom," I said, letting out a sigh of relief. "Doesn't Dad realize that I could be alone with boys any day I wanted when I'm at school? I haven't done anything crazy yet!"

Mom cocked her head at me. "Yet?"

"Strike that," I said. "Ever."

"Much better. Good cover-up, Sash." Winking at me, Mom tossed off the throw blanket and followed me to the den.

I sat back down and looked toward the tree. Dad was only a few inches down from the top—he really *was* going over every ornament!

"Hey, guys," Mom said, smiling at my friends. She

stepped around our spot and walked up to Dad. "Jim?"

"Hon, oh, right." Dad's face turned red. "The tea. It's, uh, boiling. I was looking for your favorite ornament in here. I wanted to display it in the bedroom."

"Uh-huh," Mom said, taking his arm. Looking over her shoulder at us, she mouthed, *Sorry*, before focusing on Dad again. "Let's look for that tomorrow when the kids are at the stable. I'll help you with the tea, and we can start the movie before it gets too late."

"You sure?" Dad asked Mom. "It's barely nine."

Mom nodded. "I'm already getting sleepy. I'm sure Sasha and her friends are too. They'll probably be heading to bed soon."

"Definitely," Brit said immediately. "I'm so sleepy."

"Me too," Alison added.

Dad eyed us, and I let my eyelids droop a little so I looked tired. Finally Dad nodded, and Mom followed him up the den steps. Dad shuffled off into the kitchen and Mom turned back to us.

"Stay up as late as you like," Mom said, her voice low. "Mr. Silver will be asleep in minutes, so you don't have to worry about any more interruptions."

We all smiled.

"Thank you, Mom," I said. "I love you."

"Love you, too. 'Night, guys."

My friends chorused "Good night" to Mom, and she left to help Dad in the kitchen.

"Just in case your dad becomes an insomniac, I think it's better if we stay over here," Jacob said, nodding at himself and Eric.

"Aw, you're scared of Sasha's dad! So cute!" Heather said.

"Would you want a guy messing with your dad if you brought him home for the holidays?" Jacob fired back.

His jab silenced Heather. I shot Jacob a *what are you doing?* look. Jacob knew that Mr. Fox was a sore spot for Heather. I'd witnessed some ugly exchanges between Heather and her dad. Mr. Fox was all business and didn't care what Heather had to do to be the number one rider at Canterwood. It was that cutthroat ruthlessness that had made us instant enemies. But Heather had changed. She wasn't Mr. Fox's puppet anymore.

"Let's stop talking about our dads," I said. "Anyone want to play a game?"

13

TOTES HONESTLY

Lauren

"OH, C'MON!" KHLOE STUCK OUT HER LOWER lip and made giant sad eyes at me. "It's not late, we don't have to be at the stable until eleven thirty tomorrow, *and* how many chances does a girl get to have a giant sleepover like this?"

I kept a straight face, trying to make her think I was still considering her idea. But I'd already said yes in my mind. Khloe and I were alone in my bedroom. The guys were at Taylor's house and the other girls were checking in with their parents, laying out clothes for tomorrow, and doing whatever they wanted around my house.

"I don't know," I said slowly. "Do you *really* think any-one will want to play a game?"

"YES!" Khloe bounced off my bed, ran across the room

to where I stood, skidded to a halt, and bounced up and down on her toes. "Yes, yes! They will totes want to! Please, LT!"

"Hmmm. I guess . . . okay!" I grinned. "I already thought it was a fab idea five minutes ago. I couldn't stop from letting you beg a little."

"Argh! I hate you!" Khloe said, throwing her arms around me.

"Ouch!" we both screamed at the same time.

"Khloe!" I jumped away from her.

"What?! Lauren!" Khloe's mouth hung open.

"You shocked me!" I said. "Literally. Static electricity shocked me."

Khloe covered her mouth and looked down at her fuzzy leopard-print socks. "Omigod."

We both giggled. I put up a hand, gesturing for Khloe to stay away.

"Don't come any closer," I said. "You might knock me out next time or something. Jeez."

Khloe grinned, proud of herself. "Well, I think you're rocking the I-just-rubbed-a-balloon-against-my-hair look. You're welcome."

"What?" I turned around to face my mirror. My long hair hung in its usual waves. I eyed Khloe in the mirror. "Get ready, Kinsella. Game. On."

* * *

A short (*very* short!) while later, Khloe had rounded up everyone and we were in the game room. It was a room that Becca, Charlotte, and I had always brought friends to. But once Mom and Dad heard of my plans for Christmas, they'd added a mini-fridge and snack bar. There was a pool table in the back, a dartboard on the far wall, a TV and couch and plenty of floor space.

"Okay, everyone take some of these and a pen," Khloe said. She held up the white index cards that she'd asked me for. The seven of us—Brielle, Ana, Carina, Lexa, Clare, Khloe, and I—sat in a circle on the carpet. We each had tea, soda, or hot chocolate beside us.

We all took a few index cards and one of the blue gel pens. Khloe had insisted that all the pens had to be identical. Easy, since I had a million blue pens.

"Anybody ever played Totes Honestly?" Khloe asked.

Everyone shook their heads.

"I've never even heard of it," I said.

Khloe grinned, her lips shimmering with peachy gloss. "That makes it even better. It's really easy. We're all going to take turns 'Hosting.' If it's cool, I'll be the first Host to show you how it works."

"Cool by me," Carina, who sat on my left, said.

"If I'm the Host," Khloe continued, "that makes the rest of you Bluffers. To start, I would take my index card, write 'Totes honestly . . . ,' and then finish the sentence with something that's true. I wouldn't show any of you my answer. You guys, the Bluffers, will write the same question and an answer you *think* is really true."

"Can you do an example?" Lexa asked. She sipped her hot chocolate. "Sorry! If I don't ask, I'll get confused."

"No problem!" Khloe said. "Of course. So, I'd do this. . . ."

We watched while Khloe wrote: *Totes honestly, my fave TV show is* _____.

"Now, you guys do the same and write what you think I'd say. But don't let me see," Khloe instructed.

I wrote: *Totes honestly, my fave TV show is* Sing. I kept my hand over my card while everyone else finished.

"Pass them to me, please," Khloe said. We handed her the cards, and she shuffled them around *très* fast. "I'm doing this so *you* guys can't tell my card from yours anymore. Okay, so now I'm going to read the cards aloud, and the Bluffers have to try and guess whether the card I read is true or not."

"Oh, cool!" Brielle said. She pulled her blond hair into

a messy ponytail. "This game is going to be awesome."

Everyone else chimed in with the same responses.

"Thanks, guys," Khloe said. "We can keep score or not, really. Up to us. We'll take turns playing Host, and every time make sure to start your card with 'Totes honestly.' Oh, also—if you really don't know the answer, you don't have to vote for your card. You can choose someone else's answer as yours—no one will know."

"Ooh!" Ana squealed. She sat on Khloe's right, with Clare next to her. "I have so many lines. I could play Host forever."

We laughed.

"Me too!" Clare said.

"So about scoring," I said. I paused and let a few seconds pass as my friends looked at me. "I say we keep score. First person with ten points wins. How about the loser has to do a dare of our choice?"

"OMG!" Carina said.

"LT!" Khloe said, pretending to wipe away a tear. "I'm so proud."

"Whoa, Laur," Bri said. "Brill idea! Maybe you should text Sasha and tell her that you're channeling Heather."

"No, I'm not," I said quickly. "I'm not saying we should do a mean or scary dare. Just something fun."

"Chill," Bri said, shaking her head and smiling at me. "I was totally teasing you."

I stuck out my tongue at her. "Who can we trust to keep score?"

"I vote for Carina," Lexa said.

Soon Carina had a legal pad and had written all of our names on a fresh sheet of paper.

"I think Khlo should go first, since she thought of the game," Lex said.

"Go, Khloe!" I chanted.

I looked around as my friends cheered on my bestie. Khloe sat directly across from me, then, in counterclockwise order, it went Ana, Clare, Bri, Lexa, Carina.

"Let's use these"—Khloe held up our cards—"as my first turn. Hope you guessed right, girls."

Khloe held up the first index card. "'Totes honestly'," she read, "'my fave TV show is *Reality Stars*.'"

We all started answering at once.

"False," I said.

"False," Clare answered.

"True," Lexa said.

"True," Carina said.

"False," Ana said.

"False," Bri said.

"Under each person's name, I'm going to write that answer, *T* or *F*, and then put a 'one' if that person guesses right," Carina said. She carefully recorded all of our answers.

"Next card," Khloe said. "'Totes honestly, my fave TV show is *Sing*.'"

We shouted answers as Carina scribbled on her notepad. Soon we'd gone through all the cards.

Khloe waved the index cards, smiling. "So . . . totes honestly, my fave TV show is . . . *Sing!*"

Carina crossed out and circled a bunch of things on her paper. "We have two points awarded to Lauren and Clare!"

"I almost answered wrong," Clare said. "I thought you might have put that new prep school murder mystery show as your favorite."

Khloe laughed. "I *almost* said that too. But *Sing* is still my favorite. Who wants to Host next?"

"You go," I said to Clare. "You won a point."

The group agreed with me. "Mine is, 'Totes honestly, I dreamed about *blank* last night,'" Clare said.

I scrawled down *Totes honestly, I dreamed about riding at the stable last night.*

We handed our cards to Clare, who shuffled them and read each one.

"'Totes honestly,'" Clare said, reading the last card, "'I dreamed about kissing a boy last night.'"

Khloe giggled. "Ooh, I *hope* for your sake that's true!"

Clare blushed and shook her head.

Each of us answered *true* or *false*. I called out "False," sticking to my answer.

"So, last night," Clare said, "I totes honestly dreamed about kissing a boy."

"Claaare Bryant!" Khloe said.

"Details, please!" Lexa said, laughing.

Brielle raised her mug. "To lucky Clare for dreaming about kissing last night."

Clare's face almost matched the color of her curls. "Oh, I'm *so* going to regret telling you guys that!"

"We're not playing another round until you spill, Clare-bear," Khloe said. "Who was he?"

Clare covered her face with her hands and groaned. "Garret."

"Omigod! I knew it!" I said. "You totally like him!"

"Clare, good choice of boy to dream kiss," Khloe said. She reached over to high-five her friend.

"Your dream guy is best friends with KK's boyfriend," Lex said. "How perfect is that?"

We forgot all about points, and the game changed from Totes Honestly to Garret and Clare.

14

DEFINITELY NOT
REINDEER GAMES

Sasha

MOM KEPT HER PROMISE—TWENTY MINUTES later I heard Dad snoring. Over the TV.

"I think we can all get a little closer now," I said. "My dad's out."

Heather smiled. There was that *look* in her eye. I knew it well—it meant she had an idea. Likely one that could get us in trouble, or cause someone to be embarrassed or need to spend time in therapy. Just a regular night with Heather Fox.

"Who wants to get a *lot* closer?" Heather asked.

Alison and I traded quick looks. As Heather's best friend, Alison knew what this could mean.

"What are you thinking?" Alison asked.

"I haven't played 'Guilty Party' in forever," Heather said. "You guys interested?"

"I know that game," Jacob said. "It's really fun."

The rest of us shook our heads. I trusted Jacob's endorsement. If he liked it, the game wasn't something that would get us put under house arrest for the rest of break.

"I haven't heard of it, but I'm game," Brit said. "Explain away, please."

"Each of us write a 'crime' we've committed," Heather said. "You can put down something lame like wearing stripes and polka dots at the same time out in public, but you're really playing the game when you write down something embarrassing or secret."

I swallowed. This was going to get interesting. Fast.

"Don't let anyone see what you write down," Heather continued. "But put your name on your paper. You'll hand them all to one person who's like the judge. The judge picks a card and chooses three people, one who *is* guilty, and asks them to convince the rest of us that he or she committed the crime."

"So even if you *didn't* do it, you want everyone to think you did?" Brit asked.

"Yeah," Heather said. "You want to be the best liar. Everyone but the judge gets to question the three suspects. After enough questions, they all write down their guesses. The judge collects those and the suspects are dismissed. The same judge starts the process all over again until every crime has been read."

"Then it's the really fun part," Jacob said, grinning. "The judge tallies up who guessed the right suspect the most amount of times. That person is the best 'lie detector.'"

"You guys in?" Heather asked. "Obvi, Jacob is."

Everyone nodded yes, and I grabbed pens and index cards from the kitchen.

"Who wants to be the judge?" Heather asked. "That person gets the free pass of not having to spill a crime."

We all looked at each other. I didn't want to be the judge—whoever volunteered was obvi going to get teased for wimping out and not wanting to share a crime.

"Fine, I'll be the judge," Eric said. "But to keep it fair, I'll tell you guys a crime I committed after everyone else has their turn."

"Nice, Rodriguez," Heather said, nodding. "Start writing down your crimes, people. And don't be ridic and write something dumb."

I pulled my knees to my chest and put the card on my knee. I uncapped a pen and let it hover above the paper. If Heather wanted to play, I was going to play.

Brit, Alison, and I were the first three called up. We stood in front of the fireplace. Everyone else sat on the floor or the couch and faced us.

"You are each charged with a *very* serious crime," Eric said. "The charges are, and I quote, 'I spoke to someone I shouldn't have and didn't tell my friends.'"

Not my card.

"Sasha, go ahead," Eric said.

I took a step forward. "What I did was wrong, but not telling my friends about it was even worse. This person reached out to me, and I should have hung up. But I didn't. I've been keeping it a secret since." I looked into each person's eyes. "I'm sorry. Please let me explain more when the game is over."

I stepped back in line, keeping my face emotionless.

"Alison, you're up," Eric said to her.

Alison confessed to the crime; then Brit took her turn. I listened carefully to each of them speak and watched their backs. When Alison spoke, I caught her digging her thumbnail into her palm. Either she was doing it on purpose to fake a guilty tell or *she* really had committed the crime.

The first three of us sat down and everyone wrote down their guesses. *Alison,* I scrawled.

The game continued, and no one had taken the easy way out and written anything silly. Eric had read crimes such as *I was in the headmistress's office because I'd cut English. She was all serious, and for some reason, I started laughing and couldn't stop!*

Another one of my faves was *I dropped my toothbrush in the toilet and got it out. My phone rang and I forgot to wash my hands!*

"Heather, Sasha, Callie," Eric said. "You're up. Your crime is: 'There are three words I want to tell someone but I haven't.'"

I was glad for the darkness of the room. My face got hot and it felt as though everyone was looking at me, though they were really looking at all of the suspects.

Eric had just read my crime.

Heather and Callie both lied brilliantly. Or the parts I managed to tune into were good. I felt like I was alone, standing in front of my friends. My gaze was fixed on the bowl of gold pinecones Mom had on the end table. Eric knew the card was mine. I looked quickly at him, and his face showed no signs of shock, anger, or hurt.

"Sasha?" Eric asked. "You're up."

I fumbled in my pocket and closed my fingers around a tube of Sugar Plum Fairy gloss. I applied it and gazed out at everyone.

"I—I," I started. I looked at Jacob. His kind green eyes met mine. All of my nerves vanished.

"I committed this crime," I said, starting again. "There is someone I love. I've felt that way for a while, but I've been too scared to tell that person. I was afraid he wouldn't feel the same way. Or that I'd turned into one of those crazy girls who said those words to a guy a week after dating. But I don't think I'm that girl." I took a huge breath and stared into Jacob's eyes. "Jacob, I'm guilty. I truly committed this crime. I should have told you before. I love you."

Immediately, he was on his feet. He reached me before I could even process what I'd just done. His hands were on the sides of my face and his lips almost brushing mine.

"Sasha, I love you," Jacob said, never breaking eye contact.

I wrapped my arms around his neck, pulling him *that* much closer. I kissed him and his smooth, warm lips felt good against mine. Jacob *loved* me. Jacob loved me!

We pulled apart, our arms still around each other, and both of us grinned like idiots.

"You totally ruined the game," Heather said to me. "In the *best* possible way."

Brit, Alison, and Paige were clinging to each other. Almost teary.

"Yay!" Callie whispered. She gave us a thumbs-up. "Finally!"

Eric smiled at me, then Jacob. "Nice crime, Sasha," Eric said. "I think you win."

"No," Jacob said, shaking his head. "I definitely won."

15

I'M DREAMING OF A KISS THIS CHRISTMAS

Lauren

A COUPLE OF HOURS LATER, ANA PUMPED her fist in the air. "First to ten, baby!" she said. "Game over!"

"Awesome job," I said.

Ana smiled at me. "Why, thank you. I think I'm just a good guesser. That's probably why I always do pretty well on those fill-in-the-right-circle tests at school."

My friends and I laughed. We had been playing Totes Honestly for what felt like minutes. But the refilled Cokes, second and third cups of Candy Cane Lane tea, and more hot chocolate signaled otherwise.

"Props to KK for coming up with the best game ever," I said. "I think she deserves to be crowned Official Game Chooser for all future parties."

"Agreed!" Lexa said.

"Miss Scorekeeper?" Clare asked Carina. "Who has the lowest total?"

"Wow," Khloe said, uncurling her legs. "I was having so much fun—I kind of forgot about the score. But now I totally want to know."

Carina looked at the legal pad and glanced up a few seconds later. She shifted her eyes to me. *No way. I didn't do* great, *but I lost?!*

"Laur," Carina said. "I'm sorry to say . . . you are *not* the loser."

"Mean!" I said.

Carina looked at Clare. "Clare, I'm sorry, but you scored the lowest."

"What?! Argh!" Clare shook her head at herself. "I think we should stick with Khlo on this one and go with the fact that we're having so much fun that who cares about a silly score?"

Khloe reached over to hug Clare and rock her like a baby. "Oh, bestie. Did you not hear the second part of my response?"

Clare tried to frown, but the sparkle in her blue eyes gave her away. "Okay, okay! I'm going to wash my mug. You guys come up with my dare."

She stood, smoothing her red cotton pj pants. They

had silver glitter candy canes along the bottoms. *Très* holiday chic.

I formed a huddle with Ana, KK, Carina, Lex, and Bri.

"It's obvi, right?" Khloe asked in a whisper.

"Garret," Ana said, tucking a loose light-brown wave behind her ear.

I looked over to make sure Clare was still gone. "Definitely. I don't want to do anything embarrassing, but what about a little push?"

We stopped whispering when Clare padded into the room. The six of us broke our huddle and re-formed a circle. Clare, eyeing us warily, sat back down.

"If you tell me I have to run your neighborhood in my pj's," Clare said, "I'm going to be very cold *and* very mad."

I waved my hand, dismissing the notion. "You'll be plenty warm, Clare. We promise. Let's go to the living room and I'll grab what you need."

Clare looked at me sideways but didn't say a word. She followed us out of the game room and into the living room.

"You guys chill in here and I'll be back in one sec," I said.

"Are you going to give me any hints?" I heard Clare ask the other girls.

"How long have we been friends?" Khloe asked her.

Giggling, I went into the guest room where Clare was staying and swiped her phone from the night table.

With phone in hand, I went to one of the hall closets, where Mom kept a box of miscellaneous Christmas stuff. I dug through the random assortment until I found exactly what I wanted.

"Perfect," I said aloud.

I put my hands behind my back and re-entered the living room. Clare was on the carpet in front of the fireplace with Khloe. Ana and Bri were on one couch, and Carina and Lexa sat on the other.

"Who wants to explain?" I asked.

The girls motioned to me.

"Clare," I said. "This is your dare." I put my hands in front of me, revealing her BlackBerry in its cheery yellow case and a red Santa hat complete with faux-fur white trim and a white pouf at the tip.

Clare frowned and scrunched her nose. "You want me to wear a Santa hat while I call someone?"

I sat cross-legged in front of Clare. "Close. You're going to wear the Santa hat, we'll take a pic with your phone, and you're going to send it to Garret with a holiday message."

Everyone but Clare burst into giggles.

"Guys." Clare's tone was pleading. "Please, please, puh-lease! Not Garret!"

Khloe shook her head. "Sorry, gorge." She took the hat from me and placed it atop Clare's head, adjusting it until it looked just right.

"You look *so* cute!" Carina said. "Really! I don't think this is a bad thing, Clare. Garret will think it's awesome that you put yourself out there."

"Truth," I said. "I know he likes you. The night of my birthday party was crazy, but I *did* catch Garret looking at you. A few times."

Clare tilted her head. "Really?"

"Really," I confirmed.

Clare was quiet for a minute. "Okay! Anyone have gloss?"

Brielle passed her a tube of Sephora gloss. Clare took the wand and swiped the peachy color across her lips. She dabbed a bit on her cheekbones, rubbed it in, and had an insta-glow.

"Um," I said, looking at Brielle and Ana.

"Clare, you just taught us an EBT," Ana said.

"Essential Beauty Trick," Brielle explained. "Lauren, Ana, and I have been trading those for years. Now we have a new one."

"Cool," Clare said. "I just learned that from *TeenStyle*."

I waved a hand at Khloe. "Come out of the shot," I said. "Clare, stay on the hearth. The fireplace gives off the perfect light."

I turned on Clare's camera and pointed it at her.

"You look *ridic* cute," Khloe encouraged Clare.

That made Clare grin.

"On three," I said. "One, two . . . three!"

On three, I hit the capture button. I knelt down with the phone and everyone crowded around the screen.

"Your first shot is perfect," Ana said. "Lucky!"

I nodded. *"Parfait."*

"You like it?" Khloe asked Clare.

The blush on Clare's cheeks that *wasn't* from the lip gloss gave us her answer.

"Now, what do you want to say?" Lexa asked. She lay out on her side, stretching her toes toward the fire.

"Dreaming of you," Khloe said, straight-faced.

"Khloeee!" Clare said, lightly hitting Khlo's upper arm. "Yeah, right!"

"Our first dream kiss was amazing?" Khloe tried again.

That made everyone laugh. Even Clare. I laughed so hard that my sides hurt.

"Yes, Khloe," Clare said when she had recovered from her giggle fit. "That's exactly what I'll say."

"I know! Kiss me under the mistle—," Khloe said.

"Stop!" Clare cut her off. "No. More. You've been quite helpful enough, thank you."

I passed Clare her phone, and we watched as her fingers hovered over the keypad. Suddenly she started typing. "There," Clare said a few seconds later. "How's that?"

Lexa and I read the message to ourselves. *This started as a dare, but I realized I rlly did want 2 say Happy Xmas. Not that I won't c u b4 then. ☺ C u 2mrw.*

"Niiice," Lexa said. "Send it!"

Clare took a deep breath, held it, and pressed send. "Ahh!" she shrieked. She tossed her phone away from us and onto the couch, where it landed facedown.

"What's wrong?" I asked.

Clare pulled the Santa hat over her face. "What if Garret has his phone near him right now? He could be looking at my message! Oh my God."

Khloe pulled Clare's hands down from her face. "I *hope* Garret's looking at it. It was a sweet message, Clare. There wasn't anything embarrassing about it. In fact, I'm proud of you."

Clare looked up at Khloe. "Proud of me? Why?"

Khloe sidled next to Clare and slung an arm across her friend's shoulders. "Because even though it was on a dare, *you* made the first move. That's so cool and brave. I know that I wouldn't have the guts to send a guy that I was crushing on a message first."

"I had to," Clare said, shaking her head. "It was a dare."

Khloe cocked her head. "C'mon. If you *really* hadn't wanted to do it, do you think we would have made you?"

Clare looked down at her hands, then back at us. "No. It was a good excuse for me to say something to Garret."

"Exactly," I said. "This sounds so nineties, but girl power! Now it's up to Garret. You put yourself out there in a very non-pressure-y way. I bet he's reading it now and probably scared to respond."

Carina took a sip of my favorite holiday tea—Celestial Seasonings Sugar Cookie—and tucked her legs under her. "You think boys are scared to message *us*?"

"Totes," Khloe said. She leaned back against one of the brown leather recliners. "Think about it. The pressure is really all on *them*. They're usually the ones to ask us out, so they have to deal with the possibility of rejection. We have all the power. We can ask them out or not, say yes or no."

"I never thought about it like that before," Clare said. "If Garret's reading my message, he—"

Beep! Beep!

All of our heads swiveled to the couch. Clare's phone was blinking.

"I'm *not* checking that!" Clare said. "I can't! Not yet."

Lexa got up and bounded over to the couch. "Then I will."

"Omigod." Clare pulled the Santa hat back over her head.

Lexa pressed a few buttons on the phone, and I watched her face for signs of a good or bad response from Garret.

Emotionless, Lexa cleared her throat. "He wrote back and attached a photo."

"What?" Clare asked, dropping the hat. "A photo of what?"

"See for yourself," Lexa said, a smile curling over her lips.

Clare took the phone and her eyes scanned the screen before she looked up at us. "OMIGOD! LOOK!"

Ana took the phone, and we crowded around her. There was a photo of *Garret* in a Santa hat! *Thx, C! Tay had 1 of these @ his house, 2. C u 2mrw.* ☺

"Clare!" I said. "This is awesome!"

"He so didn't have to take a pic," Bri said. "It means that he majorly likes you. And he put a smiley face. Double points."

Clare looked from one of us to the next. "You think?

He wasn't just posing in that hat to spare me from being super embarrassed?"

"Brielle is right," Ana said. "This is great! You might be kissing a boy in real life—not your dreams—before Christmas!"

"Cheers to that," I said, holding up my mug of tea.

"To kissing real-life boys, not just dreaming about them," Khloe said.

"And to Clare for sending the pic and message!" Lexa added.

"To Clare!" we all said, and clinked our mugs together.

16

#CANTERWOODTAKEOVER

Sasha

TUESDAY MORNING WAS A BUSTLE OF ACTIVITY
in my house. We'd all gone to bed super late after getting
caught up in Heather's game. I'd been too wired after my
confession to sleep. But having to drink two lattes instead of
one was a small price to pay for all the fun I'd had last night.

All of the girls took turns in the bathroom. At one
point, I was applying gloss and mascara almost cheek to
cheek with Paige, while Heather sat on the edge of the
bathtub and flat-ironed her hair. Finally I gave up on trying to squeeze into the bathroom. Pausing in the hallway,
I updated my Chatter status.

*SassySilver: 1st morning @ Safe Haven 4 Thoroughbreds!
Can't wait 2 c what we do! Mayb we'll c @LaurBell & friends.☺
#CanterwoodTakeOver*

I hurried to grab a hair tie from my room. I passed by the living room. Eric and Jacob, already dressed and looking as if they'd been ready for hours, sat on the couch. They were on their phones and talking. I caught a snippet of "Internet game" and shook my head.

"You guys are lucky," I said, putting my hands on my hips.

"How so?" Eric asked, looking up. An amused smile was on his lips.

"You can roll out of bed five minutes before you have to be somewhere and you're ready. You get dressed, run your fingers through your hair, brush your teeth—done."

"Wow. So you know our routines, huh?" Jacob asked. He traded grins with Eric. "You forgot that we use deodorant, too."

"Oh, *wow*," I said, using Jacob's word from earlier. "Sorry, that added seven seconds to your time. You have no idea what it's like in the bathroom right now. Six girls. One bathroom. Hair. Makeup. Clothes. Like I said, *lucky*."

I couldn't help but smile at Jacob as I started walking to my room. *He* loves *me!* I couldn't help chanting that in my head.

"Want us to get a camera in there and start filming?" Eric asked, stopping me. "It can be a new reality show. Six girls," he said in a TV commercial voice. "One bathroom. Who will come out alive? Find out on the next episode of *Girls Can't Share: Death by Hair* . . ." Eric paused. He looked at me. "Hair twirler tool? Curly hair wand?"

I folded my arms and jutted out a hip. "Can I help you? Better question: *Should* I help you?"

Eric hung his head. "I already totally blew my line."

I smiled sweetly. "It's okay, Eric. You're just a boy. What you were looking for, BTW, was 'curling iron.' See you in a bit!"

I exited the room, leaving both guys mumbling something about "too many girls everywhere," and I giggled to myself.

Mom dropped us off at the front of Safe Haven at a few minutes to ten. The small paved parking lot was less than half full. An old red Ford pickup truck idled in its spot. Through the window, I watched a woman in the driver's seat pull on leather gloves and a gray beanie and pick up a mug of something that steamed up the glass.

It was barely forty degrees outside, and my teeth were chattering a little after just getting out of the warm car. At least there was no wind and not a chance of snow all week. I was glad I'd layered my clothes and worn tights under my breeches. Our name tags hung around our necks—I would have forgotten mine if it hadn't been for Paige this morning. Each of us carried a helmet, too. I'd loaned two of mine to Paige and Jacob.

"Do you think there aren't a lot of adults on our shift?" Callie asked. "Or maybe most of the volunteers are dropped off like us?"

Alison shook her head and shrugged. She'd braided her hair into a purposely messy fishtail braid that hung over her right shoulder. This morning, just like me, she'd put on breeches, a thermal shirt, and an extra-heavy wool sweater. "I don't know, but this doesn't look good to me. I understand that multiple shifts are scheduled and sure, a lot of riders are dropped off, but that parking lot is *scary* empty." Alison chewed her thumbnail. "What if some of the volunteers quit already?"

"Then we'll just have to make up for them," Eric said, looping a friendly arm through Alison's.

"He's right," Jacob said. "We're not helping by standing here and worrying. Let's get inside and see what we can do."

Just when my heartbeat had started thumping way too fast over the *thought* of the Safe Haven adopt-a-thon going wrong, Jacob's words managed to calm me down. That and the swipe of Tarina Tarantino lip gloss in Neon Vanity that I applied. The bright tinted gloss made me happy just looking at the tube.

We left the parking lot and started for the entrance of the stable. The barn was older and more worn than Canterwood's stable. The main parts of the stable were painted an espresso brown, and the off-white trim amped up the warmth factor. The front sliding double doors were open and someone—there was a star on the name tag, so he had to be a coordinator—led two chestnut mares past us and toward a turnout pasture.

"Need any help this morning?" an older girl, also with a star on her name tag, asked as she approached us.

"Yes, we do," I said. "I'm Sasha Silver and these are my friends. We're here for our shift and we have our list of duties, but—" I looked at Heather.

"We wanted to double-check with someone in charge to make sure we were headed in the right direction," Heather finished.

"Sure, no problem! I'm Quinn, by the way." She stuck out her hand to each of us. "I've been with Safe Haven for years. It's the best. Thank you all so much for volunteering."

"We're so happy you had room for us," Paige said.

"Even people like me, who aren't experienced with horses."

Quinn shook her head, her long black ponytail swishing. She was dressed in well-worn fawn breeches and paddock boots, and the white helmet under her arm had dozens of scrapes. "We need all the help we can get," she said. "The holiday adopt-a-thon requires a lot of people who can do all sorts of things."

"But orientation was packed," Paige said. "Won't all of those people be enough?"

Quinn gave P a half smile. "It would—if they all came back. We have a high dropout rate with the volunteers. I think a lot of them expect to ride a racehorse and that's it. That's what one volunteer said last year, anyway. A lot of people don't come back once they see how much work actually needs to be done."

"That's ridiculous," Brit said, pressing her lips into a line.

Quinn put a hand to her cheek. "Oh, jeez. I hope I didn't scare you guys off with that info!"

We all shook our heads.

"No way," Eric said. "We're staying."

I nodded. "We'll be here for every shift and more if we can."

"You all are awesome," Quinn said. "You seem a lot

like me when I was your age. I got a degree in law just so I could help fight for the rights of horses like these. I graduated last summer, and I volunteer here almost every minute I'm not at work."

"That's so cool," Heather said. I looked over and almost did a double take. Heather Fox's eyes were wide with admiration. She almost looked . . . shy. Like she had a zillion questions for Quinn but was too intimidated to ask. *Heather. Fox.* I'd never seen her like this.

Quinn smiled. "Show me your schedule and I'll put you to work."

I traded smiles with my friends as Jacob handed Quinn our schedule. We were from Canterwood—"work" wasn't something we were afraid of.

17

SOMETIMES, THE BEST GIFTS AREN'T IN BOXES

Lauren

MY PHONE BEEPED AND I PICKED IT UP, MY palm sweating a little. It was a text from Becca.

> *Be home in 5!*

It was almost eleven, and because my friends and I had to get ready for our shift at Safe Haven, I'd stayed home with everyone while Mom, Dad, and Becs went to pick up Charlotte from the airport. We'd have only a few minutes to say hi before it was time to head to the stable. Ana had slept at home last night, and so had Brielle. Their parents wanted "bonding time." So the girls and I would meet them and the boys at the stable.

I sipped the Celestial Seasonings Tension Tamer tea

I'd made earlier. As if this was my first cup. It was my third. And a half.

I started to click off my phone when I noticed an alert signal on my Chatter app. I opened it and almost spilled tea down the front of my sweater.

"Guys! You guys, c'mere!" I yelled.

Feet pounded on the carpet and down the stairs.

"Lauren?! Are you okay?" Lexa called.

She reached my side, with Khloe right behind her.

"Sorry! I didn't mean to scare you," I said to them. They dropped their shoulders and Khloe raised an eyebrow. "Everything's okay," I added when Carina and Clare hurried down the last steps from the second floor and ran over.

"You better have, like, a new photo of a shirtless Hollywood hottie Aaron Hylend or someone equally as cute," Lexa said.

"It's better," I said. "Look!"

I thrust my phone away from my chest so everyone could see. The girls peered at the screen, and Carina's lips moved as she read the message.

"Uh, that is *way* better," Khloe said. "You're *in* now, you know that, right? *The* Sasha Silver Chattered at *you*." Khloe bowed her head, pretended to hold up a dress as she curtsied, and grinned at me.

"Please," I said, shaking my head at her. "I'm not *in* anything or anywhere. It's just *très* exciting that Sasha knows who we are. Imagine if we got to watch her ride at a Youth Equestrian National Team practice or something. We would learn so much."

"I would do a thousand math problems every night if I got to see that," Lexa said, her eyes still on my phone.

"Chatter back," Carina said.

That made me need another gulp of tea. "What would I say?" I asked.

Khloe patted my hand. "She didn't ask you to marry her, LT. Just be chill and write whatever you want!"

The other girls nodded.

"Charlotte and my family are going to be home any second," I said. I looked out the window at the driveway.

"Better type fast," Lexa said, smirking at me.

I took a *deep* breath. "Okay! Um . . ."

@SassySilver: VERY EXCITED FOR OUR FIRST DAY!!

I erased the message. "I was screaming at her," I said.

I tried again.

@SassySilver: It's totally exciting! Mayb we'll end up doing stuff w u & ur friends!

"That is so lame," I said, erasing the message.

@SassySilver: I'm sure it'll b fun. ☺ We'll c u around!

"There," I said with a satisfied smile. "How's that?"

"Perf," Khloe said. "Send it!"

"Do it!" Clare added. She started doing a weird little dance, and everyone cracked up. "What?" Clare asked, laughing. "It's the Chatter Dance!"

I pushed update just as a car door slammed.

"Good timing," I said. "And thanks for the dance, Clare. You now have to do that *every* time I update Chatter."

"Will do," she said.

I inhaled through my nose, letting the air out slowly through my mouth. I had no reason to be so insanely nervous. The person on the other side of the door was my *sister.* Yes, we'd had our not-so-very-nice moments, and we still had a lot of issues to work through, but Char was my family.

"We're going to head upstairs," Khloe said, motioning to herself and the rest of the girls. "You need time for a family moment."

"You don't have to go," I said immediately. "Char knows you're here."

"We're not going to disappear," Lexa said. "We'll be in the guest room hanging out. You can bring Charlotte up to meet us when she's settled in and stuff."

I nodded finally. "Thanks, guys."

As they headed upstairs, I grabbed my coat and slid on shoes. I opened the door, a blast of cold air rushing inside, and stepped onto the landing. I took one more breath and went down the stairs and hurried along the sidewalk to the driveway.

Immediately, I spotted brilliant blond hair flowing from under a black knit beanie.

"Char!" I called.

My sister turned away from the SUV and let go of her suitcase handle. "Lauren!"

I ran over and wrapped my arms around my sister. Charlotte embraced me back, and for the first time, we squeezed each other like we never wanted to let go. Out of the corner of my eye, I caught Becca watching us, smiling.

"Girls, let's get the luggage inside and then you can say hi, okay?" Dad asked.

Char and I pulled apart. We smiled at each other, and her beautiful blue eyes looked extra blue with the thin line of black kohl liner that rimmed them.

"It's really good to see you," I said, taking a red travel suitcase from the back of the SUV.

"You too, Laur," Charlotte said. "Thanks for helping with my stuff."

I nodded, and the five of us carried and wheeled Charlotte's suitcases into the house.

"I'll take the heavy ones upstairs," Dad said. "Laur and Becca, will you help Char with the rest?"

"Sure," I said.

Becca nodded in agreement. She took off her coat and sneakers, looking *très* cozy-chic in a white sweater with a glittery snowflake on the front and black yoga pants.

"I'll go make you a cup of your favorite tea, honey," Mom said to Charlotte. Char slid out of her wool coat and sported a Sarah Lawrence hoodie over skinny jeans. She took off her hat, running her fingers through her long blond hair. I wondered when Pantene would find Char and offer her a hair-commercial deal.

"Thank you, Mom," Char said.

Char, Dad, and I got Charlotte's stuff up to her room. We lined the suitcases up along the wall, and Dad reached out to hug Charlotte.

"We've all missed you," he said. "I'm the happiest dad on the planet to have all of my girls home for the holidays." He kissed Char's forehead and left the room.

Char flopped onto her back in the middle of her bed. Her room's color scheme was done in Sarah Lawrence College colors—green and white. Char's bed had a fluffy white comforter, white pillows, and a green iron head-board twisted with leaves and vines. Above her bed hung a gold-framed image of a gryphon—the school's mascot. I'd had to Google "gryphon" when Char had told me it was her school's mascot. I stared at it for a second—it had the head, wings, and front feet of an eagle on a lion's body. She had photos of herself and her friends in thin gold frames cascading up the wall by her closet.

"It is *so* good to be home," Charlotte said. "Finals were the worst ever." Her eyes were closed as she massaged her temples.

"We're glad you're here," Becs said. "I'm going to get your tea from Mom, Char."

I shot Becca a *what are you doing?* look. I was a little nervous to be alone with my sister, despite our friendly greeting.

"Thank you, Becca," Charlotte said.

Becca left the room, and Charlotte sat up and patted a spot in front of her. "Sit for a sec?" she asked.

I gingerly sat down. "I have to, um, leave in a few min-utes," I said. "My friends and I have to be at the horse rescue for our shift."

Charlotte smiled. "No worries. What I want to say won't take long."

C'mon, Becca, I thought. *Hurry up!*

"I e-mailed you because I'm betting you were probably nervous about me coming home," Charlotte said.

I played with the edge of my sweater, then nodded.

"I was nervous too," Charlotte said. "You and I are so much alike that it's always caused this rift between us. But I've been away. You've been away. I really, *really* want to give Mom and Dad the best Christmas present I can think of. . . ."

I looked at her as she trailed off.

"What?" I asked.

"You and I getting along. Mending our relationship and letting go of the past." Charlotte nudged my knee with her hand.

"What do you think?" she asked.

I'd never heard my sister sound so sincere. Our fighting did put stress on our parents. I wanted the small amount of times that all of us were home to be great. Not full of squabbling.

"I think we'll be able to give them an empty wrapped box and then explain their present once they've opened it," I said, smiling.

Charlotte hugged me again, and I hugged her back.

"Sorry," Becca said as she came into the room. "Didn't

mean to interrupt. I'm leaving." Becs put a Santa mug on Char's nightstand.

"You're not interrupting," I said. "I have to go, but Char has a gift idea for Mom and Dad that she probably wants to tell you about."

Smiling, Charlotte nodded. "Can we catch up a little, Becs?"

"Um, *yeah*," Becca said.

I got up and Becca took my seat.

"Laur, when you get back, I'd love to meet all of your friends," Charlotte said. "If that's cool."

I grinned. "It's totally cool."

I waved good-bye and scurried toward the guest room to gather everyone and leave. Who would have thought that giving an *empty* box might be one of the best gifts of all?

18

I FEEL LIKE
AN ELF

Sasha

I WAS BUSY READYING TO GROOM MY SEC-
ond horse of the morning—a sweet bay gelding named
Watson. He was tall, like Charm, though his bone struc-
ture was much finer and he was leaner. My phone buzzed
in my coat pocket. I pulled it out and looked at the screen.
I had a new text message.

> *Sasha, pls come to BC after the adopt-a-thon*
> *on Saturday @ 7pm. Having a little Xmas*
> *bonfire. Bring your friends! xo, Kim*

A bonfire sounded liked the perfect way to unwind after
the event. I'd get to visit Charm and hang out with everyone
at my old stable. Smiling, I put my phone back in my pocket.

"Quinn told me a little bit about you," I said to Watson. I'd just taken him from his stall and clipped him into crossties.

Quinn had gotten everyone else started with jobs too. Jacob and Paige were helping put up Christmas decorations with a group of people who, like them, weren't experienced equestrians. Quinn had said decorating the stable was so important for the adopt-a-thon, and potential adoptive people always raved over the festive feel.

Callie had been asked to feed a list of horses, so she was in and out of the feed room with different grain mixtures, depending on the horses' needs, and flakes of hay.

Alison and Brit were in the outdoor arena lunging horses. Heather had been asked to groom, tack up, and ride a horse that had been tagged as one ready to go to a home as a pleasure horse.

"Make all of the mistakes that a beginner rider might," Quinn had told Heather. "Let a stirrup iron flap for a few seconds, don't double-check the girth, drop a brush or two, really do anything you can think of to test this horse. Take note of his behavior and what scares him or doesn't. We've put him through so much already that by now he should be a safe ride for a fairly new rider."

I focused back on Watson. "So you, mister," I said,

"just came off the track a few months ago. You were fast, but not fast enough for your owners, huh?" I hugged his neck. "I know that's not true. It's their loss to have let you go, Watson. You're going to get a much better home, where you'll be the speed demon of the stable!"

Watson shifted his weight as I swiped his left shoulder with a body brush. He was barely four years old, and I couldn't let my guard down around him for a second. He wasn't mean or intentionally dangerous, but he was definitely energetic and hot-blooded. His dark-brown ears stayed pointed toward the stable exit, and he yanked on the crossties.

"Easy, shhh," I said. "I bet someone will exercise you today."

I kept whispering to Watson, trying to keep him calm. He danced in place, almost stepping on my toes.

"How's it going?" a soft voice asked. Quinn slipped under the crossties and placed a gentle hand on Watson's neck.

"He's a great horse," I said. "Is anyone exercising him today, though? I'm worried he'll kick a hole in his stall if he doesn't get a chance to stretch his legs."

Quinn scanned her clipboard, then looked back at Watson, frowning. "No one's free to ride him today. Well, no one with the experience to handle him."

"I can," I said quickly. "I'd love to ride him."

Quinn looked at me, her mouth open as she paused. "Sasha, I know from your paperwork that you're a skilled rider. Watson is fresh off the track. He's still a bundle of energy, and his exercise schedule still includes allowing him to gallop around the track with another horse. We're working on teaching him not to always feel he has to 'win,' but also giving him a sprint on the track because he'll go stir-crazy otherwise."

My entire body tingled. I wanted nothing more than to ride this ex-racehorse around a track. For a second, my silks— the outfits jockeys wear— flashed in front of my eyes. Pink and white with a glittery stripe down my helmet. Not exactly traditional, but they were my *daydream* silks.

"Quinn," I said, "I promise you that I can handle Watson. I would *never* say that if I didn't mean it. I would be putting his safety at risk—not just mine. Please let me ride him."

Quinn stared at me for what felt like hours. Finally her head dipped. "Okay."

"Thankyou, thankyou!" I said, grinning.

"Let me see who's going to be your exercise partner," Quinn said. She ran her pointer finger down the clipboard.

"Oh! Well, this works out great," Quinn said. "You'll be exercising with someone from your school. Do you know . . . Lauren Towers?"

19

IS IT COMPETITION?

Lauren

"LAUREN," QUINN, A COORDINATOR, SAID TO
me. "I'd like you to exercise ride one of the horses. Does
that sound okay?"

"Definitely!" I said. "I'd love to ride."

We had just arrived at Safe Haven. On the way over, I'd
gotten a text from Kim about a bonfire Saturday night. I'd
told everyone, and they seemed as excited as I was about
hanging out at Briar Creek.

Now, though, there was zero time to even think about
Saturday. The minute we'd walked into Safe Haven, the
coordinators had been ready for us to start our shift. Like,
immediately. Quinn had already assigned tasks to the rest
of my friends, and they'd headed off in separate direc-
tions. I was the only one who Quinn had asked to ride. It

felt like I hadn't been on horseback forever, even though I'd ridden Whisper a couple of days ago.

"Great," Quinn said, looking at a clipboard. "I'd like you to groom and tack up Reeser. He's one of the fresher horses off the track. He needs a good workout. If you are up for it, I'd like you to take him for a gallop on our track."

Excitement shot through my veins.

"That sounds great," I said. "I'd love to be on the track."

"Perfect," Quinn said, smiling. "You'll be riding with another horse and rider. The rider's actually from your school and said she knows you."

It wasn't any of my friends, so

"Do you know Sasha?" Quinn asked.

My excited feelings took a nosedive. Nerves replaced them.

"Yes," I finally answered. "Sorry. Not enough tea this morning. Sasha's a grade ahead of me."

"I gave you both serious tasks that require extreme caution," Quinn said. "I've told Sasha to let her horse gallop too, but not kick into that drive mode where he feels he has to win. It's not a race, although I want both horses to be allowed to stretch their legs."

Quinn pointed me in the direction of Reeser's stall, and I felt as though I was walking on a treadmill. I kept walking, but not getting anywhere. I wasn't worried about handling Reeser. Instead I was focused on the fact that I was about to go up against Sasha on the track. We weren't racing, but I'd be comparing my riding to hers the entire time.

I got off the imaginary treadmill and stopped in front of Reeser's stall. "Hi, boy," I said in a soft voice.

A copper-colored gelding turned his head away from a green hay net and looked at me. He had a crooked stripe down his face. His ears, alert, pointed at me. Reeser stepped up to the stall door and stuck his head out to me.

"Aw, you're a friendly guy, huh?" I asked. "You're gorgeous. Wow."

Reeser was nothing but muscle. He was trim—so fit that it was easy to tell he hadn't been off the track long.

"I'm going to get a grooming kit and tack, and I'll be right back, mister," I told him.

No one's going to be watching you and Sasha, I told myself. *So you are the one with the complex. She's not competition. It's not a race. You're partners, and you've met Sasha! She's not going to be judging your ride the entire time.*

I shook it off and made friends with Reeser while I groomed and tacked him up. I held his reins in one hand and fastened my helmet. I tugged down my blue wool peacoat and wiggled my toes in my brown paddock boots.

"Lauren?"

I turned and Sasha stood, smiling, with a beautiful bay beside her. Sasha wore a peacoat too, except hers was plum. She had fawn breeches and worn-in black riding boots. Her helmet showed evidence of a few falls.

"Hey," I said. "I didn't even hear you guys. These rubber mats are good."

I wanted to smack the top of my helmet. Like Sasha wanted to talk about *rubber mats.*

Sasha smiled, nodding. "This is Watson. Quinn told you we're exercising them together, right?"

"She did. I'm excited to go out on a racetrack. It's been a fantasy of mine, but I'm way too tall to be a jockey."

"Omigod," Sasha said. "I *dreamed* about being a jockey! I don't have the right build. Getting to race on the track is insane."

"Do you want to race?" I asked. Goose bumps covered my arms.

"No, we're not supposed to," Sasha said. "I didn't really mean race. Galloping as fast as we want, though, is pretty close."

Watson yanked the reins through Sasha's fingers, jerking her forward a step.

"Whoa," Sasha commanded.

Watson stilled immediately. He blew out a breath, clearly frustrated, and I saw hints of red inside his nostrils.

"Let's get out there," I said. "Before Watson tears your arm off."

Sasha nodded. For a second, I thought I saw a flicker of doubt or fear on her face. But this was Sasha Silver. No way was she scared. Reeser stood quietly, shifting his weight. He wasn't getting rattled by Watson.

"Just FYI, even though you totally don't need me to tell you, Watson's pretty new off the track," Sasha said. "Quinn said he's a handful. I need to let him work out his energy and do it where he was born to be, but I can't let him get out of control."

I nodded. "You won't let that happen."

"Reeser seems so much calmer, so if things get out of control, could you help me set the pace?" Sasha asked. "Only if you're able to do it safely. If not, only worry about yourself."

"If you need help, I'm there if I can," I said.

Watson let out an ear-shattering neigh. His ribs vibrated as his trumpetlike call made other horses whinny back.

Sasha and I nodded at each other and without another word led the horses toward the exit.

Reeser kept a quick walk, almost trotting in place beside me as we walked toward the track. His breath was visible in the cold air.

"Hi, girls," Quinn said, waving at us from the entrance to the track. She held the reins of an older, sturdy appaloosa gelding. "I'm going to act as an outrider in case either of you need help."

Races I'd watched on TV like the Kentucky Derby ran through my head until I remembered that outriders were sort of like pool lifeguards. Quinn wouldn't ride with us, but she would be on the track ready to get to us if we needed help. Her mount wasn't a high-strung Thoroughbred, but rather a horse that would calm the ex-racehorses. The appaloosa barely blinked when Watson tugged Sasha forward again.

"Easy, cool it," Sasha said, giving the reins a quick tug.

Reeser started feeding off Watson and reached his muzzle toward the other gelding, bumping his shoulder.

"Hey!" I moved Reeser away from Watson and made him follow me through three circles before I halted him.

"Are you guys sure that you're okay?" Quinn asked. She mounted the gray-and-white appaloosa, watching Sasha and me the entire time.

"I'm ready," I said.

"Me too," Sasha added.

"All right," Quinn said. "Warm them up, then let them go. Use your own judgment and pull them up before they overexert themselves or if they start to get overexcited. I'll be here if you need me."

I turned my attention away from Watson and Sasha. The only way I would ride well was if I focused on my horse and myself.

I double-checked Reeser's girth, then gathered the reins in my left hand. I stuck the toe of my paddock boot into the silver stirrup iron. I bounced once before pushing up off the ground and gently settling into the lightweight English saddle. I put my other foot into the stirrup iron and stood, making sure the length was right.

Parfait.

Reeser stood still, only his ears swiveling. I lowered myself into the saddle, and he jolted forward at a fast trot.

"Whoa," I said, bumping against the saddle seat and pulling him to a halt.

I knew my face was red. I'd just looked like a total beginner. I'd been warned: I had to be prepared every second.

At least Sasha and Quinn are the only ones out here, I said to myself.

Then I looked over toward the older girls.

So much for a private ride.

Brielle.

Ana.

Carina.

Lexa.

Clare.

Khloe.

Drew.

Taylor.

Cole.

Garret.

Zack.

All of my friends were lined up along the track's white fence. They weren't alone, either. Sasha's group—Callie, Brit, Heather, Paige, Alison, Eric, and Jacob—stood near the fence too. I checked my watch. It was just after noon. Lunch break.

My stomach grumbled, and not because I was hungry.

20

DREAM OF BEING
A JOCKEY: CHECK.

Sasha

MY LEGS SHOOK AS I GRASPED WATSON'S reins and a handful of black mane, and managed to get into the saddle before he crab-stepped toward Reeser and Lauren. I pulled on the reins and pressed my left boot against Watson's side, signaling him to move away from Lauren and her mount.

Watson jumped sideways as if I'd shocked him with my boot. *Your movements and signals need to be more sensitive,* I chastised myself.

I kept my hands low over Watson's neck, stilled my body in the saddle, and pulled ever so slightly on the right rein. Watson followed my cue, and we started to move through a large circle. My eyes, narrowed through Watson's ears, wandered for a second to the sight at the track fence.

Had a Chatter update gone out that I didn't know about? My friends, Lauren's friends, and several other volunteers from Safe Haven stood along the track rail. I half expected them to be betting on who would "win."

But this wasn't a race. It was exercise. Unless Watson miraculously calmed down in the next several minutes, I was going to have a hard time keeping his speed in check. I was glad that Quinn had a mount saddled up and ready to come to my—or Lauren's—aid if we needed it.

Watson faced Reeser, and I nodded at Lauren. "Ready to get them on the track?" I asked in a soft voice. I didn't want to spook Watson or Reeser.

"I'm ready," Lauren answered.

The younger rider could have been a jockey if she wasn't so tall. She was controlling Reeser without showing signs of forcing him to do anything. He was responding to her cues, and I envied her—I knew that my seat wasn't that secure when I had been her age.

We edged Reeser and Watson closer to each other. I kept Watson at a super-slow walk—wanting to make sure he was comfortable around Reeser.

"I want to let Watson feel out Reeser," I said to Lauren, not shifting my gaze.

"Good idea," she said. "Reeser is fine so far."

Neither horse was bothered by our voices. *Ah, probably because of all the noise at the racetracks,* I thought. *These guys are used to announcers shouting and noisy crowds.*

The group that had gathered along the wall, however, was silent. I spotted Jacob's red coat among the mostly black and blue ones, but couldn't look at him long enough to meet his eyes. I had to pretend the crowd didn't exist.

Lauren and I entered the track on our horses, and they moved comfortably at a walk. We kept a space of about four horses between them.

"This is like a dream," Lauren said. "Can you believe what we're doing?"

I let out a half inch of rein. Watson bobbed his head, grateful for more room. "No, I feel like an announcer is going to call our names and we're going to load the horses into a starting gate."

"Ooh, I forgot about that," Lauren said. She let Reeser walk a little faster. The chestnut moved well under her, and he was calm. "I'm a little claustrophobic. I don't know if I'd like being in that tiny space."

"It *does* look small on TV," I said. "I bet that—"

Watson threw his weight forward, pulling hard on the reins. Leather seared my fingers, but I didn't let go. I scrambled to regain the amount of rein I'd lost. Watson flattened his black ears against his head and shook it from side to side.

"Easy, easy," I called. "It's okay, boy."

Watson rose into the air, ignoring my words. He stretched his front hooves toward the gray sky, and I started slipping out of the saddle.

I am not falling off!

I twisted black mane in my fingers and pushed my own weight forward, against Watson's neck, throwing him off balance. As quickly as he'd reared, he had all four hooves on the ground. My heart thumped in my chest. I tapped my heels lightly against Watson's sides—I wanted him to keep moving forward and not try to rear again.

"Sasha," Lauren said in a quiet voice. "Are you okay?"

I didn't answer. I kept my fingers entwined in Watson's mane and used every part of my body that was in contact with his to try and feel for a hint—even the slightest clue—that he was going to rear again. But once seemed to be enough. Watson walked in a straight line and obeyed my commands.

"Now I'm okay," I answered.

"That was really scary," Lauren said. "I know you can handle it, Sasha, and you weren't scared at all. But if you want to go back and let Quinn find someone else to ride these guys, I'm cool with that."

I smiled. "You're silly to think I wasn't scared. Being on a thousand-pound-plus horse that could flip onto his back and crush you beneath him is *terrifying*. I just can't let Watson know that's how I feel. I'm okay to keep riding unless things really start to get out of control."

"Sounds good," Lauren said. "Want to trot?"

"Let's. It's time to let these boys burn off some energy."

Without any prodding from me, Watson switched from a fast walk to a trot. Reeser trotted beside us. Lauren and I posted to our horses' trots, but I knew neither of us had to. Watson's trot was the smoothest of any horse I'd ever ridden. I was pretty sure it was the same for Lauren and Reeser.

The horses' hooves churned up the loose dirt on the track, and the longer we trotted, the less Watson acted out. Lauren and Reeser kept pace with us—the gleaming chestnut was a great match for her. I knew that she had a gray mare—Whisper, I think—at Canterwood, but if she hadn't gotten her own horse yet, Reeser would make a good one.

"Canter?" I called to Lauren.

"Ready!" Lauren said back.

I sat deep in the saddle and gave Watson a little extra

rein. I pressed my knees against his sides, and he responded instantly. Simultaneously, he and Reeser started cantering. We followed a gentle turn of the track and passed a mile marker. I wasn't sure which one it was—but I knew jockeys watched them to determine how far they had gone or how much of the race was left.

Watson cantered happily, an ear forward and one ear back. His strides were longer than Charm's, even though Charm was part Thoroughbred. I barely moved in the saddle, and all I could hear were the pounding hoofbeats of the two horses and the whoosh of wind in my ears.

Reeser and Lauren kept up beside us. I looked over for a fraction of a second, and we smiled at each other.

I thought back to Callie's worries at the beginning of break—that my friends and I had to watch our backs because of how talented Lauren and her friends were as riders. I hadn't seen much of Lauren's rider friends aside from the jumping at Briar Creek. Now I was getting a front seat to Lauren's riding. She had everything a rider needed to do well at Canterwood. Better than "well." Despite that, I didn't feel threatened. Lauren wasn't a mini-Heather—a Heather back from our early days. Lauren loved horses. She loved riding. She seemed more like me than I think she realized.

Reeser pulled ahead by a half stride. Watson didn't charge after him like I expected. As a reward, I let out more rein, and with a snort, Watson increased his speed. The two horses cantered side by side.

Watson's rhythmic breathing mixed with the sounds of hoofbeats on the track made me grin.

It was time.

"Go?" I asked Lauren.

"Go!" she said.

I eased my hands up along Watson's neck and lifted myself so I hovered above the saddle. Watson seemed to almost pause for a second—as if he was testing that I was really asking him to gallop. He must have gotten confirmation, because he moved into a ground-eating gallop. I kept him in hand and didn't allow him to move to the top speed I knew he was capable of achieving.

I sneaked a peek to my left, and Lauren was bent low over Reeser's neck. The shiny chestnut's mane flowed against Lauren's face, and she smiled.

"This is awesome!" I said, hoping Lauren could hear me.

"The best!" Lauren said.

We swept past Quinn and the crowd along the rails. Watson didn't push for a faster pace. I'd given him what he wanted—a chance to run.

Lauren and I let the horses continue their controlled gallops. Sweat broke out around Watson's neck as the reins rubbed against his coat. I kept him even with Reeser, and he didn't fight me to overpower the other horse.

"Easing up," I told Lauren.

She nodded. "Me too."

I gathered the reins and slowly brought Watson down from a gallop to a canter to a trot and finally a walk. It didn't feel as if I was riding a live wire anymore. Or holding a ticking time bomb. Watson tossed his head playfully, happily.

Reeser, breathing hard, was as winded as Watson. The other ex-racehorse's nostrils flared as he breathed fast. Despite the exercise, there was a bounce in his stride.

"Wow," I said. "That was one of the best rides in my entire life."

"Oh, me too!" Lauren said, all smiles. "I still can't believe it just happened."

I edged Watson closer to Reeser and held up a hand. "To us having a chance to play jockeys."

Laughing, Lauren slapped my palm. "To us, indeed!"

21

AN EARLY
PREZZIE

Sasha

"I CAN'T BELIEVE THE ADOPT-A-THON IS tomorrow!" I said on Friday afternoon.

"It came so fast!" Callie agreed.

Dad had dropped us off at Briar Creek for a trail ride. We were walking up to the barn from the driveway. It was another cloudy, gray day. It was barely in the forties and again, no chance of snow. I still had my fingers crossed for a white Christmas.

"Was *that* Santa there last time we came here?" Jacob asked, nodding ahead. "If you guys tell me that it was, then I'm really worried about my memory."

I looked where he gestured. A Santa figurine about half my height had been placed next to the entrance door for people at the stable's front. Light-up reindeer were on the other side. Windows were covered in decals—snowflakes, snow people, and snowballs.

"Kim decorated for Christmas," I said. "Yes! She has the best decorations. I always help put them up."

"You did get to do that at Safe Haven," Brit said.

I smiled. "That was a fun day."

A few days ago I'd finished exercising a horse and had gone to the decorating committee with Jacob, Paige, Lauren, and Taylor. Even though Lauren and I weren't assigned to this area, which fell under the red experience level, we'd both wanted to get creative. We'd had so much fun going through the boxes of Christmas decorations and picking up where the last shift of decorators left off. Lauren had gotten a surprise when her sisters, Becca and Charlotte, had shown up. Both older girls weren't riders, but they definitely knew how to decorate. When we'd finished, Safe Haven looked like a winter wonderland.

"Wow," Alison said as we walked down Briar Creek's aisle. "These decorations are awesome!"

She was right. The entire stable had been decked out in Christmas decorations. A few people were still hanging wreaths on stall doors, out of the reach of a curious muzzle, and putting up colored lights.

Garland stretched from the top of one stall to the next. Clear teensy white lights were embedded in the garland. Glittery red and green ball ornaments hung on fishing line from the rafters and looked as if they floated.

The overhead sound system was tuned into the local holiday tunes radio station, and Christmas music filled the stable at a low volume.

"Tack up and meet out front?" I asked. "I'll help Jacob."

"I'll help you, Paige," Callie said.

Paige nodded her thanks. I couldn't have been prouder of my friend—she *and* Jacob were game to ride, and they had spent most of their days at a stable surrounded by horses. I wouldn't be surprised if Paige asked me to help cook meals for the homeless or something next Christmas. I smiled to myself—Paige had tasted my cooking. I wouldn't be making meals for *anyone*.

Twenty minutes later we were all astride our horses and headed toward the trails.

"Sasha," Brit said. She walked Apollo next to Charm. "We want to give you a little, tiny thank-you for everything you've done for us so far."

I scrunched my nose. "I don't need a thank-you. You guys deserve one—you're all here for me."

"No," Eric said, shaking his head. "We're here to help horses and make a difference this Christmas. That's because of you."

We pulled up the horses as we reached the edge of the woods.

Paige and Heather grinned at me. "We want you and Jacob to go on a trail ride," Heather said. "Just the two of you."

I grinned. "What? But what about you guys?"

Alison waved a gloved hand. "Puh-lease. I think we can find our way down a trail and back."

I glanced over at Jacob. He was on the other side of Brit and Apollo.

"Did you have anything to do with this?" I asked him. My tone was high and totally giving away how excited I was.

"Nothing," Jacob said. "If everyone really, *really* wants us to go, I think it would be rude for us to say no."

"Oh, yeah?" I asked, laughing. "Well, then I guess we better go."

Callie nodded. "Go. Or we will think you're rude."

Brit blew me a kiss and winked. "Have fuuun!"

I shot her a *stop it right now* look, and she burst into giggles.

"See you guys back here in an hour?" I asked.

Heather checked her watch. "Sounds good."

I eased Charm forward and Jacob did the same with Bliss, the bay mare he'd ridden last time.

"This might be one of the best ideas those guys have ever had," I said. I stroked Charm's gleaming neck with one hand as I guided him closer to Bliss.

"It's up there for sure," Jacob said, grinning. "I was hoping for some alone time with you."

"Me too," I said.

We entered the thick woods, and I angled Charm down a side path. This one wasn't used as often as the main trail that I'd taken my friends on during their first visit. The bare trees were full of chirping birds and twittering squirrels. Bleak sunlight peeked through thick gray clouds, and I was glad I'd worn my down-filled vest.

"Sasha, it's been amazing to spend so much time with you," Jacob said.

We were close enough that our boots almost brushed against each other's.

"It's been great for me, too," I said. "It's different to see you outside of campus."

"Good different, I hope."

"Very good different," I said, smiling.

Charm and Bliss walked with ease beside each other. Charm knew this trail by heart. Even though we'd been at Canterwood for a while, he hadn't forgotten his way around.

"When we played Guilty Party, you kind of stole part of my Christmas present for you," Jacob said.

"What do you mean?" I asked. I looked into his clover-green eyes.

"I was just as guilty as you. I've wanted to say 'I love you' for a while, but I was . . . scared."

"Of what?" I asked.

The horses kept a steady walk, sidestepping a downed tree and continuing along the dirt path.

"Of scaring you off. You not being ready for me to say it. Scared of you not feeling the same way yet."

I nodded slowly. "I understand. I felt the same way, Jacob. But that night, when I was standing up there feeling like I wanted to pass out because of what I'd written on that card, I looked at you."

I reached out my hand, neck-reining Charm. Jacob enveloped my hand in his.

"I looked at you," I said again. "All of my fear disappeared. I knew it was the right time. That you felt the same way. I couldn't wait another second to say it."

"I'm glad you didn't wait," Jacob said. "I was going to say it to you on Christmas, but you beat me to it."

"Sorry I stole your idea," I said, giggling.

"I'm not," Jacob said. He squeezed my hand. "I have another gift for you, anyway."

"I know it's a wonderful present, whatever it is," I said. "But in this moment, I couldn't hope for anything more."

Hand in hand, Jacob and I rode down the trail talking and laughing—it felt like Christmas morning times ten.

22

FEELS LIKE CHRISTMAS MORNING

Lauren

"GOOD MORNING, EVERYONE," LYSSA SAID. "The day we've been working for is finally here!"

I looked around at the group of people in the indoor arena. At the last day, maybe half of the first group of volunteers who had signed up was here. My friends and I stood with Sasha and the rest of our group from Canterwood. All of the older Canterwood girls had red and green ribbons woven through French braids in their hair. *Très* chic!

"First, I want to offer my sincerest gratitude to all of you who are here this morning," Lyssa added. "You are a special group of people because you have been here for the duration of our adopt-a-thon preparation. Without your help, today would not be possible."

I glanced at Bri, who stood at my right, and smiled. She did the same. My repaired friendship with Bri was one of the many good things that had come from this experience. The hours we had spent at Safe Haven had given us several opportunities to talk. We spent hours talking about the Taylor situation and I was finally, 100 percent, able to forgive her.

Break had also allowed me to spend time I'd desperately wanted with Ana. I realized all over again how much I missed her. We caught up on *every* detail in each other's lives. Ana had also gone into detail about why she hadn't told me about Bri and Taylor dating over the summer. With our talks, any residual anger I'd been holding on to had evaporated.

Spending time with these horses and thinking about their situations—how they were almost like foster kids being shuffled from owner to Safe Haven and hopefully to a forever home—made me think about how lucky not only Whisper was, but also all of the other horses at Canterwood and Briar Creek.

"Thanks to your time and dedication," Lyssa said, pulling me out of my thoughts, "potential adopters will be showing up any minute to meet horses that you've prepared. Please refer to the list of available horses with their photos on the wall behind me if you need a reminder of a horse's name. On the banquet table is an information stack with vital statistics about each horse. Each sheet contains the horse's name, age, gender, color, background, nature of the animal, and information about what kind of home the horse requires."

I knew those sheets *very* well. I'd been on printing duty yesterday and had printed hundreds of papers.

"If you have any questions or have forgotten something from the mock adopt-a-thon session we ran through yesterday, please come find me or another coordinator," Lyssa added.

A vehicle door slammed, and everyone turned toward the small window facing the parking lot.

"It sounds like our first potential adopter is here," Lyssa said, smiling. "The last thing I have to say is: Have fun! Be proud of what you've done, and let's find these horses some wonderful homes."

"Yeah!" someone cheered from the crowd.

I started clapping, and the entire group burst into applause.

Amped up from Lyssa's speech and from the energy of the other volunteers, I followed everyone else out of the arena and to the parking lot.

Car after car after *car* was backed up along Safe Haven's driveway. Almost every available parking space was full, and someone had already parked a sedan on the grass. Some of the pickup trucks had horse trailers attached and some didn't. Lyssa had said that many people often visited the horses first and came back with a trailer later if they found one to adopt.

The parking lot teemed with kids, teens, students around Char's age, adults, and even a few gray- and white-haired men and women.

"Um, I think the publicity worked," I said to Lexa.

We had each taken turns working on publicity and marketing for the event. I'd been paired up with Cole one afternoon to call the local newspaper, tell them about our event, and ask if they would run a notice a few days before the event. Amazingly, the paper had not only said yes, but they'd sent a reporter and photographer to Safe Haven. My friends and I hadn't been at the stable when the newspaper people had shown up, but the article had made the front page of the *Union Times*.

She nodded, her curly black hair tied up with a red ribbon. "Imagine if even *five* of these people adopt a horse!"

"Let's go!" I said. We high-fived, and I walked over to a girl who looked a lot like Becca, only a few years older.

Her light-brown hair was loose around her shoulders, and she had well-worn paddock boots paired with jeans. A newspaper clipping of the event's date and time was in one hand.

"Hi," I said to her, stopping just off to the side of the stable entrance. "I'm Lauren—one of the volunteers here."

"Hi, Lauren," the girl said, offering a hand. "I'm Jenn. I'm thinking about adopting a horse today."

"Oh, that's great," I said. I thought back to the questions we'd gone over yesterday that Lyssa had wanted us to ask potential adopters. "What's your background with horses?"

Jenn tucked the clipping into the pocket of her navy wool coat. "I've been a rider since I was six—Western and English. I'm a student at the University of Connecticut, and I've got two quarter horses that I show for pleasure."

I nodded, already liking Jenn.

"I keep my horses at my parents' barn," Jenn continued. "There are a few acres of land and plenty of room for another horse."

"Do you want another horse to show?" I asked.

Jenn shook her head. "Actually, I want to adopt a horse as a companion for my other two geldings. I'm plenty busy showing my boys and since there's extra room, I'd love to rescue a Thoroughbred that can't be ridden either due to injury or whatever reason."

I almost dropped my jaw. "Wow. That's so kind of you."

"Thanks, but the horse would be doing me a favor. I'd love to have another horse to groom and care for."

"Let's go inside," I said. "Do you have a preference for a mare or gelding?"

We walked into the stable, and I fought the urge to do a cartwheel. If only every person here was like Jenn. One Safe Haven horse was about to become very lucky.

"Either one," Jenn said. "As long as he or she is friendly toward other horses."

"Let me grab a list of horses that meet your requirements," I said. "Then you can meet them, if you like."

"Sounds great," Jenn said, smiling.

I hurried down the aisle and ducked inside the indoor arena. I scanned the table and picked up four flyers—two mares and two geldings—with their names and a head shot. All of them had red Xs next to "Able to Ride," a summary explaining why, and a smiley face next to "Herd Friendly."

I took the flyers and found Jenn stroking the neck of a gray who'd stuck his head out of his stall.

"These are four horses that can't be ridden," I said. "They were all injured on the track or during training. That paragraph"—I pointed to it—"goes into detail about what happened, how their injury was treated, and if further treatment is required."

"This is great," Jenn said, her eyes on the papers.

"I'll give you a few minutes to read about the horses. Then you can meet as many of them as you like," I said.

"Great! Thanks, Lauren." Jenn sat down on one of the benches we'd set up for today's visitors and began leafing through the papers.

I wanted to stay nearby but not hover, so I walked a few stalls away. Farther down the aisle, Drew held the lead line of a feisty black yearling who danced in place as Drew talked to a tall man in a baseball cap.

"Excuse me." A red-haired guy approached me. "I just spoke to one of the coordinators, who pointed you out to me. Lauren, right?"

"Yes, sir," I said, shaking his hand. "How may I help you?"

"I'm Ross Barker. Kelsey, the woman who's helping me, told me that you would be able to get me information on any available mares that were for intermediate or advanced riders. I've got a sixteen-year-old daughter who doesn't know that she's getting a horse for Christmas."

"That's only the best present ever," I said, smiling. "Let me go grab those papers for you. I'll be right back."

In the arena, Callie was at the table, gathering papers.

"Hi, Lauren," she said with a smile.

"Hey, Callie," I said. "I love your ribbons!"

The ribbons stood out against her raven-colored hair. "Thanks! We all did each other's hair."

"Great idea," I said. "It's so festive."

"You and your girlfriends look pretty Christmassy too," Callie said.

I reached up and touched the poinsettia hair clip just behind my ear. "Thanks! They were a surprise for all of us from my mom."

"I didn't see any of your guy friends wearing theirs . . . ," Callie said, grinning.

"We tried," I joked. "The best we could do was get them to wear red and green."

"Ha—that's what Jacob and Eric did too. Boys."

Callie shook her head and picked up another paper. With a little wave, she exited the arena.

I focused on the flyers and ended up with six mares that fit Ross's guidelines. Back in the aisle, I found him and handed him the flyers. "These are mares that fit what you described," I said. "If you need anything else, please let me know."

"Thank you, Lauren," Ross said. "I'll go over these with Kelsey."

He walked away, and I decided to give Jenn a couple more minutes. I moved out of the center of the aisle and stood next to a tack trunk in front of an empty stall. *I wonder if that horse has been adopted!*

"Laur."

Cole reached my side, smiling. He looked *parfait* for the event. He'd paired a forest-green coat with a red wool sweater. *Magnifique!*

"Hey! How's it going?"

"Amaze!" Cole said. His cheeks were flushed against his pale skin. "I showed an older mare to this retired guy who wanted a horse to basically just pet and love." Cole laughed. "And act like a lawn mower."

I giggled. "That's so cool! I hope she gets adopted."

"Me too." Cole held up crossed fingers. "Oh, there he is with Lyssa. Later!"

I left my spot near the stall and walked over to Jenn.

"Just checking on you," I said. "Are you interested in meeting any of the horses?"

"This guy, Alaric, grabbed my attention right away,"

Jenn said. She held up the flyer with a photo of a black gelding with a white star on his forehead. "I'm familiar with tendinitis. Looks like Alaric's case is too severe to race, but not bad enough that he can't live a comfortable life romping around my fields."

"Alaric's a sweet guy," I said. "I groomed him a few days ago. His stall is this way."

Jenn followed me down the aisle. As we walked, I noticed more and more of the stall doors were open and the roomy stalls were empty. *Please, please let those horses be adopted*, I thought. *Santa, that's my wish this year.*

We reached Alaric's stall, and the four-year-old gelding's head was over the door. He pricked his ears at Jenn and me. Alaric's conformation was flawless, but it wasn't his gorgeous features that made it easy to fall in love with him. It was his response to attention and his calm, curious demeanor.

"Oh, you're a nice guy, huh?" Jenn crooned at Alaric as the gelding rubbed his forehead on Jenn's shoulder.

"It amazes me how gentle and loving he is despite what he's been through," I said. "It makes me sick to think that someone was willing to almost give him away to a slaughterhouse."

Jenn's jaw tightened. "I can't even stomach that thought," she said. "People who use, abuse, and throw away animals are disgusting. I'm so grateful for Safe Haven and all of the organizations like it."

"I wish every horse will get a home today, but I know that's asking for a lot."

Alaric lipped at Jenn's sleeve, and she grinned before petting his neck.

"Try to remember that every horse who doesn't find a home today will be safe here," Jenn said. "There will be another chance for them."

I nodded, Jenn's words making me smile.

"Would you like to take Alaric out of his stall?" I asked. "We can find a quiet place for you to walk him around and get to know him."

"I'd love to."

I took a royal-blue cotton lead line from the hook near Alaric's stall and clipped it to the ring under his chin. He backed up like a gentleman while I opened the stall door, then followed me out.

"He's very easygoing," I told Jenn. "Want to lead him?"

"Absolutely."

I handed Alaric's lead rope to Jenn. The Thoroughbred pranced beside her, and I stood back as Jenn led Alaric through several circles and figure eights. She halted him, picked up each hoof, and checked his teeth and ears.

"They've all been vetted prior to today," I said. "Last week, they were shod and dewormed, too."

"That's great," Jenn said. She smiled at me, but she only had eyes for Alaric.

He's got a new home! I cheered in my head. Unless something completely unexpected happened, I just knew Jenn was going to take him. She was scratching under his chin, and the almost blue-black gelding flapped his lower lip.

Both Jenn and I laughed.

Jenn took her eyes off Alaric and met my gaze. "Where do I sign?" she asked.

"Really?! Oh, yay!" I clasped my hands together.

"I'm already in love with him," Jenn said. "I hope I meet all of the qualifications."

I stepped forward to pat Alaric's neck. "I'm sure you will. If you can tear yourself away from him." I grinned. "Lyssa, who's standing at the first banquet table, is the person you need to see. She'll get you the paperwork and go through the adoption process."

"Thank you so much, Lauren," Jenn said. "You're an incredible volunteer. I can't thank you enough for setting me up with Alaric."

I blushed. "I just pulled the right paperwork. It's an early Christmas present for all of us—especially you and Alaric."

Jenn nodded and handed me the lead line. "I guess I'll have to get a bigger tree to fit him under it."

With that, Jenn squeezed my forearm and headed off to talk to Lyssa.

I threw my arms around Alaric's neck, standing on my tiptoes to reach him. "Congratulations, beautiful boy! You're going to your first real home. Jenn is going to spoil you and take such good care of you—I know it."

I led Alaric back to his stall to await the final verdict from Lyssa. Something told me, though, that Alaric was going to have a very, *very* merry Christmas.

23

HORSES = BEST STOCKING STUFFERS

Sasha

I MADE MY WAY BACK FROM A TRAILER WHERE I'd helped load my first adopted horse. I felt like I was floating across the driveway. I'd seen at least three other horses loaded into trailers, and it was barely eleven. There were still at least a dozen people talking to volunteers, filling out paperwork, or talking to a coordinator and getting to know a horse.

I spotted Lauren—her smile couldn't have been wider. She walked out of the stable next to a black gelding led by a beaming older girl. The horse's legs had been wrapped for travel. A warm red-and-black-checkered blanket was buckled at his chest, covering him from withers to rump.

"Good news?" I asked, slowing and smiling at her and the other girl.

"*Fantastic* news!" Lauren said. "This is Jenn, and she adopted Alaric." Lauren placed a hand on the gelding's neck as Jenn drew him to a halt.

"Congratulations!" I said to Jenn. "I've learned how seriously Safe Haven takes matching its horses to the right people. I'm sure you're going to be very happy with your new horse."

The black gelding held his head high. His giant brown eyes were wide and warm. There was something about the star on his forehead that made me smile.

"I love him already," Jenn said.

Alaric bumped Jenn's arm with his muzzle. "I think he already knows that," I said, laughing along with Jenn and Lauren.

"Happy holidays," I said to Jenn. "And the same to you, Mr. Alaric." I touched the gelding's muzzle, then gave Lauren a thumbs-up when Jenn started to lead Alaric forward.

Omigod! Lauren mouthed.

I waved, grinning at her, and looked for anyone who might need help. Near the application table, Jacob and Paige were stapling applications. They kept passing the stapler back and forth—almost unable to keep up with the papers Lyssa kept handing them.

A gray-haired man in jeans and a puffy green coat stood

in front of the corkboard at the wall at the entrance of the stable. The board had photos of all of the horses available for adoption. Brit had been one of the volunteers who had helped arrange the photos. The board was decorated with garland along the top edge, and the cork had been sprayed with green and gold glitter before the pictures had been glued onto the board.

"Hello," I said, walking up to the man. "I'm Sasha, a volunteer with Safe Haven. Do you have any questions that I might be able to help you with?"

He turned to me, wrinkles forming around his kind brown eyes as he smiled at me. "Hello, Sasha," he said. "Nice to meet you. My name is Tedd Orson."

"It's nice to meet you, too, Mr. Orson," I said. "How can I help you?"

Mr. Orson ran a hand over the back of his neck. "Please call me Tedd," he said.

"Tedd," I said, smiling.

"Honestly, I'm not here to adopt a horse," Tedd said. "I want to contribute to Safe Haven in another way, and I wondered if you could help me with that."

"I'd be more than happy to," I said. There was just *something* about Tedd that made me feel as though I needed to speak to him away from the commotion of everything going on around us. "If it's okay with you, we can go to one of the quiet, private offices and speak."

Immediately his shoulders dropped, and he nodded. "Please."

Once we were inside Lyssa's office, I half closed the door and motioned for Tedd to take a seat in one of the chairs across from Lyssa's desk. I pulled a chair away from the wall and sat across from him, grabbing a notebook and pen from Lyssa's desk.

"I've been meaning to come to this event for almost a decade," Tedd said. "I'm afraid I've been too much of a coward."

I didn't know what to say. Or do. This was *not* anything at all like what I'd expected him to say.

"Well," I said after a pause. "You *are* here today. That certainly counts."

Tedd looked at his lap for several seconds and cleared his throat. "My wife used to be an equestrian," he said.

"Oh," I said. "Are you?"

"No," Tedd said quickly—almost harshly. "I mean, I was, but I'm not any longer." His tone softened. "Ten years ago, my wife died in a riding accident."

I sucked in a breath so fast that it made a tiny *whoosh* noise. "Oh my gosh. I am so sorry."

Tedd nodded. "Thank you, Sasha. I'm sorry too, not only for the loss of my wife, but of my behavior since her passing. My wife was a passionate equestrian who loved everything about horses. She couldn't spend a day without them. She taught me to love them too."

He smiled, and I forced myself to smile despite the deep sadness I felt.

"My wife was killed during what had always been a routine cross-country ride," Tedd said.

The pain in his face and eyes was visible.

"Sir," I said. "Please don't feel that you have to explain. I can't imagine how painful that must be."

Tedd's eyes met mine. "I appreciate your kindness. It's time, though, that I tell my wife's story. I haven't spoken of it since the year it happened, and I became somewhat frozen in time. Hopefully, today, that stops."

I nodded. "I understand," I said.

"My wife, Hillary, was riding her favorite mare on, like I mentioned, a familiar course at our stable," Tedd continued. "I wasn't jumping, but I followed my wife along the course to exercise my own gelding and spend time with my wife." He cleared his throat again. "Hillary and her mare approached the second-to-last obstacle—a fallen tree. I don't know why, but her mare refused the jump.

Hillary was caught off guard, and she went over the tree and landed on the other side."

I covered my mouth and bit the inside of my cheek. It would not help if I cried. It didn't seem right to interject with another "I'm sorry," either.

"I dismounted and ran to her," Tedd said, his eyes glazed over. It was as if he was back on that course. "She was unconscious. At the hospital, she was found to have a broken neck and brain damage. She had to be on life support and was in a coma for a week before I let her go."

Tedd shifted in his seat.

"Mr. Olson, I can't even begin to pretend to understand what you must be going through," I said. "It must be incredibly difficult to be at the stable."

"It's easier than I thought," Tedd said. "I sat in my car for a long time before coming in. But once I was here, I felt a sense of calm. Hillary would want me to be here. Since her passing, I've erased horses from my life. I'm not in a place of mind to own a horse today, or maybe ever, but I would like to offer a monetary contribution to Safe Haven."

"I obviously didn't know your wife, but I'm sure this is something she would be incredibly proud of you for doing," I said. "Please know that whatever amount you give will go one hundred percent to the animals in Safe Haven's care. We do not charge adoption fees—we only ask adopters to contribute what they are able. Your donation is so appreciated."

Tedd reached into his coat and produced an envelope. He handed it to me. "Sasha, I cannot thank you enough for listening to me. I'm thankful that you approached me and were so kind to hear me speak of Hillary."

"I'm truly honored that you shared something so personal with me," I said. "Thank you so much for your donation. May I send a thank-you note to the address on the check?"

Tedd stood, a genuine smile on his face. "You're welcome, although I actually owe this organization a thank-you. The address is actually from my company—not my home. I'd like to keep my donation known to as few people as possible."

"Your secret's safe with me," I said. "I promise."

"And I promise to be back next year."

I saw Tedd to his car and walked back to Lyssa's office. I found the ledger we were supposed to use to record donations. I wrote *anonymous* in one of the spaces. There were dozens of other listings for ten, twenty, one hundred dollars—they all added up. I slid open the envelope and took out a blue check.

"Oh my God," I said aloud.

I read the amount of the check again. And again. And again.

One hundred thousand dollars.

"Tedd," I said out loud. "Thank you. I know, somehow, that Hillary's proud."

Hours later I gathered in the arena with the rest of the Safe Haven volunteers. Lyssa, standing on a mounting block just as she'd done the first day, held the donations ledger in her hand. She had mud flecks on her boots, tendrils of hair had escaped from her ponytail, and she looked happy but exhausted.

"Please, everyone," Lyssa said. "Give yourselves a round of applause!"

Cheers broke out in the arena. I clapped and grinned at Paige, who stood next to me. Lauren was on my other side. Somehow, the Canterwood group always managed to come together whenever possible. I'd really gotten to like having the younger students around. I hoped that wouldn't change once we got back to Canterwood.

"Today we broke a record for the number of adoptions," Lyssa said. "We found homes for twenty-two horses! That's nearly half of our horses who were up for adoption."

"Yeah!" someone whooped from the other side of the arena.

We clapped again. That number was fantastic! I hadn't known what to expect, but *twenty-two* horses going to loving homes was beyond exciting.

"I couldn't have asked for a better group of volunteers," Lyssa said. "I sincerely thank each and every one of you for your time, energy, and efforts that you have put into these last couple of weeks."

Lyssa held up the red ledger. "This," she continued, "has all of the financial contributions we received this holiday season." She motioned to someone and stepped down from the mounting block.

Quinn took Lyssa's place. "Hi, everyone, I'm Quinn," she said. "I tallied up the ledger, and no one except for me knows the total of the donations we received."

She grinned, looking down at Lyssa. "This year, Safe Haven for Thoroughbreds received one hundred nine thousand dollars."

"What?" Lyssa's shriek echoed throughout the arena.

I smiled to myself. I hadn't told anyone—not even my friends—about Tedd. I wasn't planning on sharing his story either. It was something Tedd had trusted to me, and I planned to keep it to myself and be able to look Tedd in the eye next year, knowing I'd done the right thing.

"I didn't miscalculate," Quinn said, laughing. "Someone, who chose to remain anonymous, donated one hundred thousand dollars, making that our single largest donation ever."

"Wow," Paige said. "That's incredible!"

"It's amazing," I agreed.

"One hundred percent of all the money raised goes right to the care of these horses," Quinn said. "I don't want to keep you here any longer. I know you must be as tired as I am. Thank you, from the bottom of our hearts, from all of us at Safe Haven. I hope you all have a very, *very* merry Christmas!"

24

KARMA

Sasha

"SASHA, MAY WE TALK TO YOU FOR A MOMENT, please?" Mom called. "Your father and I are in the kitchen."

I tugged down the creamy-white sweater that I'd chosen to wear for tonight's bonfire. It was just after six, and we were all getting ready.

Brit and Callie, both sitting on my bed, looked at me when I faced them.

"That sounds like I'm in trouble," I said, whispering. "Right?"

"No," Callie said. She looked at Brit, then back at me. "Maybe! But you didn't do anything that we don't know about, right?"

My mind raced through everything that I'd done today. I couldn't think of anything that would make Mom or

Dad angry. I'd stayed at least five feet away from Jacob and Eric at all times since we'd gotten home, Lyssa had nothing but praise for my friends and me when my parents had picked us up, and there hadn't been time for me to get in trouble.

"Sasha?" It was Dad this time.

"Coming!" I called.

"We'll be here," Brit said. "You didn't do anything—we're probably totally reading into their tones."

"I hope so," I said.

I left my room, and as I walked to the kitchen, I slicked on a coat of Merry Berry gloss. Mom and Dad were seated at the small round table in the breakfast nook area.

"We know you're getting ready for Kim's," Dad said. "This won't take long." He motioned for me to sit across from him and Mom.

I pulled out one of the wooden chairs and slowly sat down. Under the table, I rubbed my sweaty palms on my jeans. Mom's and Dad's faces gave away nothing.

"Mom, Dad," I started. "I don't know why you're mad, but I promise I didn't—"

I stopped when they both smiled at me. *Grinned*, actually.

"Oh, honey," Mom said, laughing a little. "I'm sorry

we scared you. You didn't do anything wrong, and you're not in trouble."

I let out a giant breath of relief. "You both had me so nervous!" I said. "What's going on?"

"Sash," Dad said. "Your mom and I wanted a moment alone with you. We wanted to tell you how proud we are about what you've done over the break. You orchestrated this entire volunteer event with your friends. You've spent almost all of your time at Safe Haven over the past week, sacrificing your own free time that you could be spending with friends or riding at Briar Creek."

I sat back in my chair. "Dad, thank you."

"Your father is right," Mom said. She cupped her hands around the snowflake mug in front of her. "All of the effort you put into this, sweetie, hasn't gone unnoticed. I've always known how much you deeply care for horses, but it has never been clearer to me than recently."

Tears stung my eyes. I blinked fast—I'd just finished my makeup and was not going to have smudgy raccoon eyes.

"Sasha, it's not Christmas, but Mom and I wanted to give you a gift a little early this year," Dad said. He looked at Mom, and she nodded. "We know how hard you're training for the YENT—both you and Charm. A few weeks ago, your mom and I spoke to Mr. Conner at length about your riding future."

"You did?" I asked. I wanted to say more like *Did he say I was doing well? Is he happy with my progress?* But those two words were the only ones I was able to utter.

Mom smiled at me. "Don't worry," she said in a teasing tone. "We did our best not to say anything embarrassing."

Smiling too, I rolled my eyes. "I hope not!"

"Mr. Conner mentioned," Dad said, "among other things, that it's not uncommon for a rider to have more than one horse when they are training and competing at the level where you are now and where you're striving to be."

I stared at him, not getting what he was saying. I had Charm. Charm was my perfect dream horse. Besides, it wasn't as if my parents could afford to buy me another horse. I'd never ask that of them.

"Sasha, your dad and I talked it over, and we would love to give you the opportunity to adopt a horse from Safe Haven," Mom said.

I think my heart stopped. Then it started beating out of my chest.

"WHAT?!" I shrieked.

Mom and Dad laughed, holding each other's hands on the tabletop.

"We're proposing this," Mom started. "You are incredibly busy with school, lessons, and Charm. We fully recognize that. However, when the time comes that you feel you're ready to take on the responsibility of a second horse, if that's next year or five years from now, we want you to know it is something we would love to give you. This is a chance for you to rescue a horse in need and either have a second horse to use for pleasure riding or a second horse to train for showing."

"Oh. My. God. Omigod. Omigod." I shook my head. "Are you *serious*?!"

Mom and Dad nodded.

"You deserve it, honey," Dad said. "We're so proud of the young woman you've become. We know that you'll feel when the time is right to introduce a new horse into our family."

"Omigod!" I shoved back my chair, almost tipping it over. I rushed around the side of the table and threw my arms around both of my parents. "Thankyouthankyouthankyou! I can't believe it! This is the best Christmas present!" I squeezed Mom and Dad, then let them go.

Mom reached out and touched my cheek. "Like we said, you deserve it, Sasha."

I caught my breath as the news sank in. A new horse. Another one to love and train and care for.

"What you guys said means so much to me," I said. "I can't wait until I'm ready to adopt a horse. There are so many at Safe Haven that deserve amazing homes. Right now, you're right—my life is full with school, riding, and everything else." I smiled. "Plus, Charm is *all* the horse I need and more. I know that one day I'll be ready to open my heart to a horse in need. Thank you, really, for giving me that opportunity."

I hugged my parents again, then saw the clock behind them.

"We've got to leave, like, now!" I said. "Dad, are you still up for driving us to Briar Creek?"

He nodded and waved me off to go get my friends.

I half ran down the hallway and skidded to a stop in my doorway. Brit and Callie, wide-eyed, looked at me.

"Is everything okay?" Callie asked.

"You're not in trouble, are you?" Brit questioned.

"We're still going to the bonfire, right?" Callie asked.

I grinned. "To answer your questions, yes, no, and yes! Dad's ready when we are. Let's go, and I'll tell you what just happened when we get to the bonfire. I want to share it with everyone at once."

"Um, this sounds like a big deal," Callie said, getting up and sliding into her coat.

I shot her a playful grin. "It's bigger than big. It's like, all-of-the-snowflakes-during-a-snowstorm-combined big."

Despite nonstop questions from everyone during the entire ride to Briar Creek, I didn't say a word about my surprise present. I kept the secret as if telling my friends now would ensure coal in my stocking for Christmas.

25

LET IT SNOW, LET IT SNOW, LET IT SNOW

Lauren

"MERRY CHRISTMAS, WHISPER," I SAID SOFTLY. Entering the stall, I locked the door behind me and slid my arms around her neck. A green-and-red-checkered blanket was draped over Whisper's back and hindquarters. "I got here as soon as I could," I added. "Mom just dropped us off after the adopt-a-thon ended. I had to come say hi to you before the bonfire."

The rest of my friends were visiting their horses too, or had gone to help Kim with the bonfire. I squeezed Whisper, then let her go. I moved by her head and ran my hand under her chin, her soft whiskers tickling me.

"Are you having a good vacation?" I asked Wisp. Her ears pointed forward and she breathed into my hands. "You'll be here for a few more days, girl. We have New

Year's, and then you and I will both be going back to Canterwood."

I'd been so busy with the rescue and having so much fun with my friends that I hadn't realized until now that I missed Canterwood. A lot. It was great to be home and see my parents and sisters, be in my hometown, and visit Briar Creek, but Canterwood was home too. It hadn't hit me until now.

"We're home for Christmas, but we'll be going to our other home very soon," I said. "Get some sleep, beauty. I'll see you soon."

Whisper blinked at me and nudged my coat pocket.

"Oh! You smartie," I said. "I almost forgot your Christmas treat."

I dug into my pocket and pulled out three apple-and-maple cookie treats. Mom had bought them from an organic farm, and I'd given some to everyone before we'd left my house.

I uncurled my fingers, offering one treat, and Whisper snatched the cookie off my palm. She crunched loudly and bumped my hand for another.

"Hey," I said, giggling. "You almost ate a finger. Take it easy."

Whisper lowered her head a little, almost as if she was

apologizing. I offered her the second cookie, and this time she ate like a delicate lady.

"Last one," I said. Whisper's gray, black, pink, and white lips took the cookie, and she blinked as she munched. "Good, huh?" I asked. She bobbed her head.

I kissed her muzzle. "Good night, again. I'm going for real this time."

I left the stall, latched the door behind me, and walked down the aisle. All of the horses were tucked away in their stalls and blanketed against the cold winter night. I exited out the side door and grinned. Finally!

Giant gorgeous snowflakes danced through the air. I raised up my arms and twirled in a circle, laughing. It was about time for snow! That made the evening *parfait*.

"Twirly girl!" Khloe called.

I laughed harder and Khloe ran over, grabbing my hand.

"C'mon, LT!" she said. "You have to see the bonfire."

Snowflakes stuck to my eyelashes. An orange-and-yellow glow flickered as we hurried alongside the barn. Smoke became visible in the air through the snowflakes, and I smelled wood burning. Khloe and I rounded the corner, reaching the back of the stable, and we found our friends.

All of our friends. Not just the people in our group. But the nicknamed Sasha & Co. The older students weren't just people we went to school with or knew from one holiday of volunteer work. They had become our friends. And opening a giant bag of marshmallows was Kim. It wouldn't be a Briar Creek bonfire without her.

The flames covered a half-dozen giant logs, and sparks flew high into the sky. Heather waved at me from across the other side. She was barely visible over the tall flames. Sasha and Callie laughed as they roasted marshmallows.

"Want one?"

I looked over at the familiar voice. Drew, his face glowing from the fire, held out a perfectly toasted marshmallow on a stick.

"I'd love one. Thank you," I said. I slid it off the end of the stick and popped it into my mouth. "It's perfect," I said through sticky lips.

"I grabbed this stick for you," Drew said. He handed it to me. "Kim was upset before you got here. She bought roasting sticks for tonight and couldn't find them. Lucky for her, I've grown up using *real* sticks, and so has Callie. We both went to the edge of the woods, gathered enough for everyone, and presto—roasting sticks."

"Aw," I said. "I'm so glad you and Callie helped. Let's put these sticks to work!"

Soon I'd eaten enough marshmallows to lull me into a sugar coma. Drew and I snuggled next to each other on a log-turned-bench. Khloe and Zack had their arms around each other's waists as they stared into the fire. I bumped Drew's knee with mine.

"Look," I said in a whisper.

Clare, looking Christmas chic in a red beret and matching wool coat, was hand in hand with Garret.

Drew followed my gaze and grinned. "I don't think they'll have any trouble finding some mistletoe."

I frowned. "Not sure about that. I haven't seen any tonight."

"Really?" Drew asked. He shifted on the log, then raised his arm in the air.

"What are you—?" I looked up, and a sprig of mistletoe hung from a red ribbon around his finger.

My face grew warmer, without help from the fire. I locked eyes with Drew—his so ocean blue.

"We *have* to follow tradition now," Drew said. "I'm sorry, Lauren. There's no way around it."

I sighed, pretending to be upset. "If there's no other

option. I wouldn't want to mess with a Christmas tradition or anything."

Before I could say another word, Drew lowered his arm, dropped the mistletoe, and put his hands on the sides of my face. His cool fingers sent chills over my body. We leaned forward and gently touched our lips together. When we pulled apart, I slipped my hand into Drew's. We stepped closer to the bonfire, and the flames warmed my skin. Next to us, Khloe and Zack held hands too.

Even though it was the end of our time at Safe Haven, it was the beginning of lots of things. In a few days, we would all be counting down to the New Year, and we'd return to Canterwood to finish seventh grade.

Through the light snow and the flames, Sasha had her arms wrapped around Jacob as they kissed. They pulled apart, still holding hands, and grinned at each other.

"Merry Christmas."

I froze at the sound of that voice.

It *couldn't* be.

26
SECRET SANTA

Sasha

MR. CONNER WAS AT *BRIAR CREEK*! I STEPPED forward and hugged him. "Mr. Conner! I can't believe you're here!" I said.

He hugged me back, smiling. "How could I miss a bonfire on a snowy night like this?"

"Let me get you some hot chocolate," Paige said, dashing off.

That was Paige—always the perfect, polite hostess.

"How did you know we were here?" Eric asked Mr. Conner.

"Kim was kind enough to inform me about tonight," Mr. Conner said. "I'll tell you all of the details, but I'd like to address my younger students at the same time. It's wonderful to see each of you."

Paige, mug in hand, came over and offered it to Mr. Conner.

"Thank you, Paige," he said. "This smells delicious."

"It's not from a packet and water," I said. I shot a proud smile at Paige. "Paige made it from scratch."

"I've heard that you are quite the chef," Mr. Conner said. He took a sip of the hot liquid and smiled at Paige. "What I've heard is true. This is fantastic!"

Paige ducked her head. "Wow, sir, thank you so much."

Mr. Conner took another sip, and Kim came up to him.

"I'm so glad you could make it," she said, shaking his hand.

They moved away from our group and stood off to the side, heads bent together as they talked. It was beyond weird to see my ex-coach talking to my current instructor.

"Okay, Silver," Heather said, folding her arms. "Either you spill your secret now or I'm going to turn *you* into a marshmallow over the fire."

I giggled. "Hmmm . . . okay!"

I looked at the faces of all of my friends—Eric, Jacob, Callie, Brit, Heather, Alison—and couldn't remember the last time I had felt this elated.

"When my parents called me into the kitchen," I said, "I thought I was in trouble." I wanted to give a little backstory, since only Brit and Callie had been in my room when it had happened. I explained what my parents had said, dragging it out a little until *I* couldn't stand it for another second.

"My mom and dad said that when I'm ready—*whenever* that is—I can adopt a horse from Safe Haven!" I almost screamed the sentence.

"Sasha!" Brit said.

"Wow! Merry Christmas!" Jacob said, kissing my cheek.

"Omigod!" Callie said. She clasped her mitten-enveloped hands together.

"You're kidding!" Alison said.

Eric one-arm-hugged me. "You totally deserve it! Wow!"

"Thanks, guys," I said, bouncing on my toes. "I'm super excited. I'm not ready for another horse yet. I can't even imagine having two right now, but just knowing that one day I can rescue one is amazing."

"Somewhere out there, a horse doesn't even know it yet," Alison said, "but he or she just got the best Christmas gift a horse could ever want."

27
MERRY CHRISTMAS!

Lauren

SASHA HUGGED MR. CONNER. HE SMILED AT her and her friends, and they all started talking.

"I can't believe he's here!" I said to Drew.

After a couple of minutes, Mr. Conner left Sasha and joined Kim. He shook her hand and they talked. I couldn't hear them over the crackle of the fire and the chatter of everyone else.

"This is so crazy," Drew said. "Mr. Conner is part of Canterwood. I guess that I kind of thought he never left the campus."

I giggled. "I know. Me too."

I stayed next to Drew, chatting with him and enjoying the warm fire on my face.

Shoes crunched in the inch or so of snow that had quickly accumulated on the ground.

"Mr. Conner," I said, almost hopping up and down. "What are you doing here?"

I didn't know what to do—having Mr. Conner at Briar Creek was *crazy*. It must have been even more of a treat for Sasha. Briar Creek had been her old stomping grounds longer than it had been mine.

Mr. Conner smiled as my friends and I gathered in front of him.

"I thought it was only right that I pay a visit to this evening's festivities," Mr. Conner said, a mug of hot chocolate in one hand. "After all, almost all of my seventh and eighth grade riders are here." He nodded to Taylor. "And their friends."

That made Tay smile.

"Admit it," Khloe said, grinning. "You came because we're your favorites!"

"Khloe!" I hissed. She would *never* say that at Canterwood. I think she'd had one too many marshmallows already.

Mr. Conner fought back a smile—I could tell. He tilted his head and looked at Khloe. "I came, Khloe, because I want to support my riders after the tremendous work they have done at Safe Haven. I received a phone call raving about the work done by the students of Canterwood. I am truly impressed and proud of each of you."

I bit my bottom lip. Mr. Conner wasn't one to dole out compliments. When he gave us one, it was something to savor.

Beside me, Khloe's giddiness slipped away. In the firelight, she blinked back tears.

"Sasha," Mr. Conner called. "Please join us over here with your friends for a moment."

Sasha, Callie, Brit, Heather, Jacob, Paige, Alison, and Eric walked over from the other side of the fire, filling in holes in my group of friends.

"I want to take a quick moment to speak with you all," Mr. Conner said. "Then you deserve to get back to enjoying the evening."

Drew slipped his hand into mine. I squeezed his as we looked at Mr. Conner. Our riding instructor had come *here* to talk to us. There was something less intimidating about him. Maybe it was the red beanie over his black hair, or the fact that he wore a gray wool coat instead of a Canterwood Crest jacket. Or maybe it was because Mr. Conner had come to us.

"When Kim told me about the bonfire tonight," Mr.

Conner said, "she invited me to attend and asked that I get back to her with my answer after I checked my schedule." Mr. Conner's eyes roamed over each of us. "I didn't need to call Kim back. I gave her my answer immediately. At Canterwood, you young students, those of you who ride and those who don't, are put under tremendous pressure. Both academically and whatever sport or extracurricular activity you're part of."

I caught Taylor's eye and smiled at him. He did the same back. Snowflakes continued to fall around us. The bonfire was the only source of light aside from the glow coming from the stable. It felt as though I was in a snow globe.

"Attending and excelling at Canterwood is not an easy task," Mr. Conner continued. "Each of you had every right to rest, sleep in, go out with friends—whatever you chose—during the holiday break. Instead you decided to take your time and help horses in need."

A tear dripped from my cheek, and Khloe wiped her nose.

Mr. Conner shook his head. "I don't think any of you realize how far the volunteering you've done will go. You changed the lives not only of horses, but also of the people who took them home. You boosted spirits of other volunteers, and I know, without having been present, that you lifted each other up."

I looked over and my gaze stopped on Sasha. She was already looking at me. I gave a single nod, and she did the same back.

Mr. Conner raised his white mug with candy canes in the air. "I toast each of you tonight. I am proud to be the instructor of most of you and a faculty member to those who don't ride. I am beyond touched by your combined efforts this Christmas." He smiled. "As I've heard around the stable, 'Sasha and Co.' and 'Lauren and Crew,' I wish you all health, happiness, and a holiday just as wonderful as the one you gave to countless horses and people this year. Cheers!"

Mr. Conner nodded and took a sip of his drink. We all burst into applause. I sniffled, wiping tears from my cheeks.

"Here." Callie, smiling through her own tears, handed me a tissue.

"Thanks," I said.

I squeezed Drew's hand. "I'll be right back."

"Don't be too long," he said, smiling at me.

"I won't."

I left his side, weaving through the other people. I

stopped in front of Sasha. It was as if she was already waiting for me.

Tears dripped from her cheeks onto the snow. Without a word, we hugged each other.

As I held on to the older girl, I thought about everything I'd gone through since I'd first heard her name. Before Briar Creek and Sasha Silver, I was a girl who was on her way out of Horse World. Sasha gave me a dream to chase. Now I was at Canterwood, with the best friends I could ask for, a kind, sweet boyfriend, and a horse I loved more than anything.

Sasha and I let go after a final squeeze.

"Thank you," I said, still teary.

"For what?" Sasha asked, snowflakes on her long eyelashes.

"For inspiring me when you didn't even know you were. For being someone that I could look up to and not compete against. For letting me take the reins. Most of all for being with my friends and me this Christmas."

Sasha bowed her head. She took in a ragged breath. "That's so sweet of you, Lauren. I want you to know that you and your friends have kept me on my toes at school. You're all incredibly talented, and I have to stay at the top of my game. I have you to thank for that. All of that aside,

I can't think of any other people that I'd want to spend Christmas with."

We turned our heads at the same time—everyone else had formed a circle around the bonfire.

"Dashing through the snow," they started to sing.

Sasha and I laughed.

"C'mon," Sasha said, grabbing my hand and pulling me toward the fire. "I want to show you my singing skills that make dogs howl."

I giggled, letting her lead me to the group. ". . . in a one-horse open sleigh," we both sang.

I looked around at everyone as we sang. This was the most perfect Christmas ever. I couldn't think of a single present that I wanted. Everything that I needed was right here.

Joyeux Noël!

See where it all began. . . .

CANTERWOOD CREST

TAKE THE REINS

MY PARENTS' SUV ROLLED INTO THE SCHOOL'S parking lot, past the imposing, ivy-covered wrought-iron gates. I had seven types of lip gloss in my purse and not one was Canterwood Crest Academy worthy. Peach and lime—too summery. Marshmallow and sugar cookie—too Christmassy. Reluctantly, I settled on strawberry.

"Mom," I whispered, dabbing gloss on my lower lip—desperate situations really amp up my lip gloss addiction—"are you sure about this?" The rearview mirror caught my reflection. My naturally tan face was pale and I'd slathered on so many coats of lip gloss, my lips had turned cotton-candy pink. Oops.

"You're going to be fine, Sasha. You were a great rider at Briar Creek!" Mom turned in her seat to look at me.

She tucked a strand of golden-brown hair—the same color as mine— behind her ear.

I waved my hand toward the window. "*This* is not Briar Creek," I said. "I'll be lucky if I make the beginner team here."

"You're an excellent rider," Dad said, pulling into a parking space and cutting the engine. "Don't even talk like that."

Parents are required to say stuff like that so they don't ruin their kid's self esteem. I'd seen an *Oprah* about it.

I tried one of those deep-breathing exercises from my yoga DVD. In May, when my acceptance letter had come from school, I'd taken up yoga. The thought of switching schools and riding for a new stable had been enough to give me major stress. But I couldn't do any worse here than I had at UMS—Union Middle School—in my hometown of Union. Maybe I'd make real friends here. *Breathe in, and then out. In, out.*

"All right, Sash," Dad said. "Let's go."

Reluctantly, I opened the door and took in the scene around me. Everything looked different, bigger some-how, than when I'd toured the campus in April. Beautiful stone buildings with climbing ivy, rolling green hills, lush trees with not one dead leaf to be found. And, best of all, a gorgeous, dark-lacquered stable ahead in the distance.

"Smile! Say hi to Grandma and Grandpa, honey," Dad said, shoving his camcorder in my face. "This is Sasha's first day of seventh grade. Wave to the camera, Sasha."

"Dad!" I hissed. Oprah would so totally disapprove of this! I reverted to my yoga breathing. In, out. In, out.

He beamed. "Sasha's first day at boarding school. I remember when—"

Oh my God. "Dad! Stop filming!" I slammed my palm over the lens. "Not. Now."

"Oh." Dad lowered the camcorder and switched off the blinking red light. "Sorry."

Mom read the instruction sheet for students coming to school with horses. "It says to unload your horse in this lot," Mom said. "And follow the signs to the stable area."

At least there were signs, since I probably wouldn't remember the way after five months.

Dad put away the camcorder and helped me unload my horse. Charm pawed the trailer floor—eager to get out. He had been in the trailer for two hours.

Charm, with nostrils flaring, backed down the trailer ramp. "Please behave," I whispered to him. He pranced in place and huffed as he eyed his new home. His chestnut coat glistened, his gold halter rings flashing in the sunlight. Charm was acting like a yearling instead of an eight-year-old gelding. I touched the tiny silver horse charm on the bracelet my parents had given me for good luck last night, our last night together before Canterwood.

"We'll go park the trailer and find you in the stable when we're done," Mom said.

"You're leaving me alone?"

"Oh, honey," Mom said, squeezing my shoulder. "You'll be fine. And we'll be right back."

"Promise?" I asked.

She nodded. "Promise."

My slick hands could barely grip Charm's lead line. Deep breath in, deep breath out. "Ready, boy?"

My lips felt dry. I dug in my pocket for my strawberry gloss and globbed more on. Together, Charm and I followed a sign that read STABLE, with an arrow that pointed down a grassy path. Iron signs directed riders to cross-country courses and trail riding paths. As we approached the stable, the familiar scent of horses, hay, and grain soothed me more than my breathing exercises or lip gloss ever would.

Wow, Canterwood is even more gorgeous than I'd remembered, I thought, surveying the gleaming paddocks. The lush grass looked as if someone had cut it with fingernail clippers. There wasn't a clump of horsehair or a wisp of hay out of place. Even the stones around the bushes by the sidewalks looked polished.

This place made Briar Creek look like a dollhouse-size operation. I still couldn't believe I'd been accepted to Canterwood and was about to start riding for their nationally recognized riding program!

Charm tugged me forward. "Easy," I murmured.

Just then, a *boom* came from the parking lot. At the same moment that I realized it had just been a car backfiring, my hand shot out to grasp Charm's halter. With a snort, he reared up toward the bright blue sky. The lead line seared my palms as it slipped out of my hands. I stumbled backward and made a frantic swipe for the end of the rope, but Charm bolted forward before I could grab it.

Oh my God, this couldn't be happening! In the distance, I could see Charm's lead line dangling between his legs. He could seriously hurt himself if he got tangled in the rope.

"Charm!" I yelled, sprinting after him. He galloped toward a cluster of students and then swerved to avoid them. He flew by the paddocks and headed for the arena, his hooves pounding the ground in quick beats.

"Loose horse!" I screamed.

Charm's ears swept back in fear. The whites of his eyes were visible, even from far away. Charm quickened his pace to a flat gallop. Thirteen hundred pounds of glistening chestnut zoomed around the grass.

"Here, Charm!" He slowed to a fast canter and turned toward a much darker chestnut Thoroughbred in the arena. The horse's shoulder muscles rippled under his shiny coat. A slight girl with blond hair that peeked out from beneath a black velvet riding helmet was riding the Thoroughbred.

"Watch out!" I yelled to the girl. But if she heard me, she didn't show it.

Charm flew past the Thoroughbred and knocked over a row of orange cones lined up on the outside of the arena. A cone tumbled right into the Thoroughbred's path; he reared and stretched high into the air. For a second, it looked like he would tip backward onto the girl.

My breath caught. All I could do was stare. The girl flipped off her horse's back and landed in the arena dirt.

Oh. My. God.

This was my worst nightmare.

"Charm!" I almost didn't believe it when Charm finally slowed into a trot. I grabbed his lead line with shaking hands. His sides heaved and the whites of his eyes receded as he began to calm. I pulled him into the arena entrance, ignoring my burning palms. We ran over to the girl who hadn't moved since her fall.

"Oh my God, are you okay?" I asked. Charm stood still next to me and lowered his head.

"Where's my horse?" the girl asked, her voice surprisingly strong for someone who had just had a serious fall.

"Right over there," I pointed. "He looks okay," I said, hoping that was true as I looked over to where he stood at the far end of the arena. The girl struggled to sit up.

"Wait," I said. "Should you sit up?"

The girl wiped dirt from her eyes.

"What can I do?" I asked.

"Just help me take off my helmet."

My trembling fingers unfastened her chin strap and I lifted the helmet from her head. "I'm so, so sorry. Please let me go get help." Out of the corner of my eye, I saw a dark-haired girl duck under the fence and grab the Thoroughbred's reins.

"Mr. Conner is coming, Heather," she said, leading the Thoroughbred. Charm lifted his head to eye the new horse, who stood quietly and peered down at his rider.

"Thanks, Callie," the blonde—Heather—said.

"Did you hurt anything?" Callie asked.

Heather wiggled the fingers on her left hand. "This arm."

"Is Heather's horse okay?" I asked Callie.

Callie's dark brown eyes flickered over Heather and then toward me. She felt the horse's legs. "I don't feel any heat. Aristocrat seems fine to me."

My old instructor, Kim, had taught me that, too. If Callie felt any heat, Aristocrat could have sprained or pulled something.

"Thank God," Heather moaned. "We have a show in a month."

"Thank you so much for grabbing him!" I said to Callie. "I can't believe that happened on my first day!"

A tall man with thick, dark hair strode over. I recognized him immediately from the Canterwood Crest Academy website: Mr. Conner, my riding instructor. And he definitely wasn't happy.

"What happened?" he asked, kneeling down to check on Heather.

"My horse got loose, sir," I confessed, my voice shaky. "He spooked and I couldn't hold on to him."

"Who are you?" Mr. Conner asked, raising his eyebrows.

"Sasha Silver. I'm new this year." I wondered if I would set a school record by getting expelled on my first day.

Mr. Conner felt Heather's arm from her shoulder to her fingers. "Nothing feels broken. But let's get you to the nurse, Heather, just to make sure."

Heather clutched her right arm. "It hurts, Mr. Conner."

Mr. Conner motioned to Callie. "Callie, please take Aristocrat back to the stable, untack him, and be sure he's fed."

"Yes, sir," Callie said. "I saw what happened. It really *was* an accident."

I mouthed a silent *thank-you* to Callie and she smiled in return before leading Aristocrat out of the arena.

"I'm feeling kind of dizzy," Heather said. "Could I sit for one more second?"

"Of course," Mr. Conner said, kneeling beside her. "Take a few deep breaths."

What if she had head trauma? How could I tell Mom and Dad that in the ten minutes they left me alone, this happened? No way would yoga breathing be enough to calm them down if I got expelled my first ten minutes at Canterwood.

"Were you not taught how to control a spooked horse?" Mr. Conner asked. "You're not here to learn the basics."

I couldn't believe this! First days were for good impressions. Charm and I had been practicing harder than ever lately. We'd worked all summer on form and jumping—sometimes thirty hours a week.

"It happened so fast," I said. "I wasn't able to catch him."

Charm shifted his weight and his ears drooped. Mr. Conner helped Heather to her feet. When they started walking, I noticed she wasn't clutching her arm anymore.

"I expect you and your horse to be on your best behavior for the rest of the week, Ms. Silver," Mr. Conner called back over his shoulder.

I exhaled. "Noises like that never scare you, Charm," I whispered. "What happened?" Charm blinked and gave me his trademark sad puppy eyes. "We caused trouble in our first fifteen minutes, boy. Not a good start." He lowered his head. "It's all right. Let's go find your stall."

Charm and I approached the stable entrance when a girl with curly hair asked, "New rider, right?"

I nodded. "I'm Sasha and this is Charm."

"I'm Nicole Allen," the girl said. She patted Charm's shoulder. "Don't worry about it," she whispered. "No one will remember this tomorrow."

"Do you know where I should take Charm?" I asked her, recognizing an ally.

"I'll show you," Nicole said. Charm and I followed her into the stable.

I tried not to compare Canterwood to Briar Creek once I was inside the stable's main aisle—it felt disloyal. But this place was even nicer than the National Equestrian Club we had visited in Washington, D.C.! The aisles here were wide, the stalls were enormous, and no one was riding in jeans. I almost did a double take when I saw "Charm" on the gleaming gold nameplate on the stall door. The box stall, with light wooden boards, looked brand-new.

"I've got to go practice," Nicole said. "But I'll see you later."

Charm sniffed his new blue water bucket and lipped a few pieces of hay from the hay net. I fumbled in my pocket for my pink cell phone and pressed speed dial four.

"Hello?" Kim said.

"I haven't even been here a full half hour," I croaked into the phone. "And I've already humiliated myself."

"No," Kim said, her voice soothing. "What happened?"

"Charm got loose," I said.

"Oh, dear," Kim said.

"He spooked another horse and a girl fell."

Kim gasped. "Was she hurt?"

"Yes. No! I don't think so. She walked away on her own, but she was leaving for the infirmary."

"That doesn't sound too serious," Kim soothed. "It's only the first day. By tomorrow, something else will happen and no one will remember that Charm got loose. Believe me."

"I don't know," I said, as Charm started to nose my boot. I couldn't be mad at him when he looked so scared. He was new, too, and probably afraid of his new home. "Maybe I should have stayed at Briar Creek."

"Sasha, I loved having you here, but I taught you everything I could. We both know you want to grow as a rider."

"I know," I said quietly.

"I'm so proud of you, Sasha. And you can call me anytime you need to talk. Okay?"

"Okay," I agreed. "Thanks, Kim," I added, and said good-bye.

Charm nudged my back and I threw my arms around him. "It's going to be okay," I soothed. "We can do this." I reached under his jaw and tickled his hairy chin the way he liked. Charm flapped his lower lip up and down. It made a suction sound when it hit the top of his mouth. I laughed. "Thanks, boy. You always make me feel better."

"Sasha?" Mom called from behind the stall door. "Wow! This is such a nice space for Charm."

"I know, isn't it incredible?" I asked.

Dad glanced at me sideways. "You look upset. Everything okay?"

If I was going to make it, I couldn't be crying to my parents about every little thing. "Everything is fine. I'm just excited to see the dorms."

"Let's go, then!" Dad said.

ABOUT THE AUTHOR

Jessica Burkhart (a.k.a. Jess Ashley) writes from Brooklyn, New York. She's obsessed with sparkly things, lip gloss, and books. She loves hanging with her bestie and watching too much TV. She is also the author of the Unicorn Magic series (2014) and the novel *Wild Hearts* (2015). Learn more about Jess at www.JessicaBurkhart.com. Find everything Canterwood Crest at www.CanterwoodCrest.com.